# IVAN
## and the
## American Journey

# IVAN
## and the
## American Journey

Myrna Grant

Christian Focus Publications

*To Jenni and David as they begin their journey
with love.*

Copyright © 1988 by Myrna Grant
Published by Christian Focus Publications in 2001
This edition published in 2006
by Christian Focus Publications Ltd.,
Geanies House, Fearn, Tain, Ross-shire,
IV20 1TW, Scotland
www.christianfocus.com
ISBN 1-84550-131-4

Cover design by Andrea Raschemann
Black and White illustrations by
Jos. E DeVelasco
Printed and Bound in Denmark
by Nørhaven Paperback A/S

Myrna Grant has travelled widely in what was the Soviet Union
and has experience of writing for children's TV and radio. She
is now an associate professor in communications at Wheaton
College, Illinois. She has many published works.

# CONTENTS

# The Prize

A fresh wind was blowing across the Moscow River. The summer had been short and hot, the streets clogged with buses full of tourists from all over the world. Now there were fewer buses on the wide roads. Ivan breathed deeply, filling his lungs with the cool air as he hurried across Komsolmolsky Avenue toward Gorky Park. A few leaves spun in the light breeze, rimmed with the gold of coming autumn.

At the entrance of the park, a small crowd had gathered around the morning's copy of Pravda posted on the entrance bulletin board. People were eager to read Pravda these days since Comrade Gorbachev had brought so many changes to the Soviet Union. Now it was possible to read news never before permitted. Ivan wanted to get close enough to see the newspaper, but the crowd huddled together, resisting anyone trying to shift a little closer to the front.

Every year Ivan came to Gorky Park on the last day of summer vacation, the day before the school year started. It was his farewell to summer. He loved watching the old men huddled around the stone chess-boards in the park, elbows on the edge of the chess tables, chins cupped in hands, unmoving, as if they also were made of stone. At this time of year, the little lakes in the park were as still as mirrors and

anyone who walked over the bridges spanning them could look across the water and see the feathery reflections of young trees.

Ivan tried to fight a rising feeling of dread that was taking hold of him. Tomorrow was the first day of September, the first day of school. There would be a new teacher who would be displeased because he did not wear the red scarf of the Communist Young Pioneers. A familiar worry returned. Every year there was the danger that he might be cut from the soccer team because he was a Christian. Christians were not considered model Soviet citizens and were rarely allowed to participate in Young Pioneer activities like sports. Only the fact that Ivan was an outstanding player kept him on the team. But one never knew when a complaint might force the coach to remove him.

Ivan sighed. The year ahead looked unpromising. And today his best friend Pyotr was late for their last meeting in the park. A stone splashing into the water a few feet from his bench startled Ivan. He looked around to see Pyotr's familiar grin.

Pyotr plopped down on the bench beside Ivan.

'So, did you see the paper today?' he demanded, stretching out his legs in front of him and looking straight ahead at the water, a mischievous smile playing around the corners of his mouth.

Ivan shrugged. 'Nobody would let me close enough.'

'Too bad, Ivan. It was very interesting today. I read it at home.'

'I don't' know whey you're always so cheerful when school starts, Pyotr! It's unnatural.'

'For one thing, I don't have to worry about soccer as you do. And not being a scholar like you, I don't care if my teacher doesn't like it that I am Christian. If she grades me hard, it doesn't make that much difference. I only aspire to pass my exams. I don't have to be the best, like you.'

'I don't have to be the best!' Ivan threw a few blades of grass at his friend.

'In history, you do!'

'All right, history. But not everything. Maybe history can get me into university. And especially now, with Comrade Gorbachev's glasnost – maybe Christians really will be able to go to university.'

Pyotr suddenly jumped up, pulling Ivan to his feet and almost knocking him over with a huge bear hug.

'What are you doing?' Ivan's yell was muffled in Pyotr's shirt.

'I can't stand it!' Pyotr exploded. 'Ivan! Ivan! You are going to America! You won the All-Moscow history prize! All the prizewinners are going to America for five weeks on a school exchange program. It's in the paper today. You are going to America!'

Ivan stared at Pyotr. 'I won the All-Moscow prize?'

'Yes, of course. But you're going to America! It's in the paper.'

Ivan's open mouth shaped itself into a slow smile.

'I don't believe it. My teacher entered my essay? I don't understand. Every year my essay is returned: 'Not acceptable for the contest because you are not a Young Pioneer.' How could I have won?'

Pyotr clutched his head in despair and put his face close to Ivan's. As if he were speaking to someone deaf he mouthed the words one by one. 'You-are-going-to-America, Ivan. For five weeks! Your essay was entered! Your essay won!'

Ivan sat down and then stood up. 'When? No! America?' Both boys began to laugh crazily.

An old grandmother babushka, pushing a chubby toddler in a stroller, frowned at the noise. 'Behave, you foolish boys!' she commanded.

Ivan gulped down his laughter. 'I'm sorry, grandmother,' he managed before bursting out in a new wave of hilarity. Pyotr was holding his sides helplessly. The old woman shook her head in disapproval and passed by.

'Come on!' Ivan called over his shoulder to Pyotr.

The boys raced to the entrance of the park and to the posted copies of Pravda at the gate. The earlier crowd had thinned.

Panting and trembling, Ivan stared at the front page. As he read, his face became pale with excitement.

The headlines shouted, 'Ten All-Moscow Prizewinners to Study in America.' An old feeling of fear clutched at him as he saw his own name in the paper. Poppa always said that Christians were to live quietly and were not to bring attention to themselves. And here was his son's name on the front page of Pravda!

The boys made their way home, Pyotr beaming with pride and excitement, Ivan with a look on his face halfway between terror and overflowing joy.

# Excitement at Home

Katya was watching at the open window of their apartment. When she saw Ivan running along the street toward home she leaned out over the ledge. 'Ivan! Hurry! Hurry!' she shouted needlessly, her shiny dark braids bobbing in her excitement.

Ivan burst through the door, gasping for breath. He was surprised to see both Momma and Poppa at home. Momma was smiling broadly, shaking her head affectionately at Ivan's flushed face and rumpled shirt. Poppa caught Ivan in a hug, thumping him on the back as he held him. 'So you know!' he exclaimed with each thump. 'So you know all about it!'

Katya was jumping up and down. 'America! America! America!' she kept shouting.

Momma shook her head at Katya in alarm. 'Stop that! Quietly, quietly!' she warned with a pointed glance at the door to the hall and the open window.

'Pyotr told me in the park,' Ivan panted, when his father released him. 'Then I saw it in the paper. I didn't even know my essay was entered.'

'Oh, Ivan, you'll get to ride in an aeroplane! And you'll see skyscrapers and drink Pepsi-Cola and you'll see rich capitalists and criminals on the streets!'

Ivan was not paying attention to Katya. His eyes were full of questions. Momma sat him down on the sofa and gave him a glass of water. 'We are so proud of you, Ivan. It is a great honour to win the All-Moscow prize in history.'

Ivan gulped down the water gratefully and set the glass on a nearby table. Katya knelt on the sofa beside him, juggling excitedly. Momma and Poppa sat down, too.

'But what about America?' Ivan's voice had returned to the hushed tone they used indoors. 'I mean, will it cause any problems? Will they really let me go?'

'Many things are changing,' Poppa began. 'Today at the factory, the foreman called me in. He had been notified that a son of one of his workers was travelling to America on a school exchange program. Even the son of a believer! He asked me if you would make any trouble.'

'Ivan wouldn't make trouble!' Katya exclaimed indignantly. Momma leaned over and patted Katya's hand.

'I told him you were a loyal Soviet citizen,' Poppa continued. 'I was very surprised that you had been allowed to win a prize. This has never happened before. But I said nothing about that. I told him that there was nothing to fear from you. He warned me that things would not go well for me at work if there was any trouble. Then he told me to come home and talk with you. I am to report back to him in the morning.'

'And it was the same thing at my work,' Momma smiled as if to say it was not important. 'Only I was not excused early as your Poppa was. I only got home a few minutes before you, Ivan.'

'But will they really let me go? A Christian?'

'Of course. Since it was in the paper, it has already been decided.' Poppa turned the radio on. It was a precaution against any possible 'bugging' of the apartment. Vigorous folk music filled the room. In spite of the music, Poppa lowered his voice. 'I think it must be that the international exchange program in America has requested a religious student to be part of the Moscow group. In the West there is much

17

concern about human rights. It is certain that the idea did not come from our government. But, all the same, it is now important to the government to show that there are 'no problems' with religion in the Soviet Union.'

'Poppa, that's not true,' Katya whispered in protest. 'We know that still there are many problems.'

Poppa pulled one of Katya's braids playfully. 'I know, little Katushka, but this is what Comrade Gorbachev has said, and I think the authorities will be quite happy that a Christian student has been given the prize and will be sent to America.'

For the first time, Ivan hoped that it was all true. 'America,' he said slowly. 'Where in America will I be going?'

Poppa pulled a letter out of his pocket. 'Your notification was sent to my foreman at the factory. He gave it to me after his talk.' Poppa unfolded the letter carefully. 'Stephen Academy in Vermont.' Poppa handed the letter to Ivan.

Ivan's hands were shaking. Katya giggled and tickled him so he couldn't read. 'Momma! I can't read!'

Momma stood up. 'Katya, we need to start supper. Leave Ivan to read his letter.'

Before long the welcome smells of supper wafted out of the kitchen. Katya slowly carried a tureen of cabbage soup to the table. Momma brought a plate of tomatoes and cucumbers and black bread and glasses of tea. It wasn't until Poppa had asked the Lord to bless the food and Ivan dipped his first spoon into

the soup that he realized Momma had said nothing about the journey.

'Momma, aren't you glad that I am going to America?' Ivan asked with a happy smile. Her answer surprised him.

'Ivan, things are very different in America. Have you thought about that?'

'Of course. That's what is so exciting. Things are very different there. For one thing, Christians don't have to be quiet about their faith. They can do anything for the Lord they want to. And there are Bibles and Christian books and young people's meetings!'

Momma took a sip of tea. 'America is a dangerous

country, Ivan. There are many killings there and gangs of young people that attack on the streets. There is uncleanness there, for anyone to see, in magazines and books. I'm not sure it is good for a Russian young person to be in such a place.'

'How can it be as bad as we think when there are so many Christians and churches? And so many Bibles? Perhaps it is not the way we have been told at all!'

Poppa finished his soup and pushed the bowl away, reaching for the family Bible that he kept carefully wrapped in newspaper. As he lifted the Bible out of the paper, he gazed fondly at his family. 'In all this excitement, we must not forget that the Lord is our shepherd. It is for him to lead and for us to follow. He is also our shield. He will protect us from evil. If it is God's will that Ivan make this amazing journey, then God will guide and protect along the way. Ivan is in the care of God. He is safe anywhere, is he not, my dear wife?'

Momma nodded gratefully. 'Of course. It is just that it is a long journey, and I am a mother.' She smiled at Ivan and Katya.

Poppa looked thoughtfully at Momma's face, lit as it was by her smile. 'It may be, of course, that in the end, a reason may be found to prevent Ivan from making this journey. There are improvements just now in our Soviet life. But things can change back just as quickly. We have seen that happen in the past.'

Ivan nodded. There had been changes before in

Soviet history. In the time of Comrade Khrushchev new programs to move the country forward had begun. Then Khrushchev had fallen from power and the old ways returned.

'I hope Comrade Gorbachev remains in good health for many years,' Ivan took a big bite of bread and chewed it quickly. 'It is a fine thing that he allows such exchange programs.' A slight shadow troubled Ivan's eyes. He glanced at Momma. 'Of course, it is a very long way.'

Poppa turned the pages of the Bible until he found the passage he was looking for: 'The eternal God is our refuge,' he began, 'and underneath are the everlasting arms.'

# A Warning

The new teacher, Maria Kharchevna, was standing by the entrance of her classroom, checking off the new students on a list tacked on the front of the door. As Ivan approached, he looked at her curiously. She was a tall woman of about 30, her blond hair pulled back from her face and forehead, with penetrating deep-set blue eyes.

'Good morning, Comrade Teacher,' Ivan greeted her politely. 'I am Ivan Nazaroff.'

Maria Kharchevna gave Ivan a piercing look. 'Good morning, Comrade Nazaroff. I wish to see you at the end of the day. Please come to my desk before you return home.'

A sting of fear caught his voice and Ivan cleared his throat carefully. 'Certainly, Comrade Teacher.' He took his seat and watched the other children in the class file in slowly. The room seemed to be a blur of white blouses and shirts, proudly accented by the splash of the red scarf tied jauntily under each neat collar. As a Christian, Ivan did not wear the Young Pioneer red scarf which signified belief in the Soviet state and disbelief in God. Always he hoped it might happen that there would be another Christian in his class, but it had never happened. He was the only one without the bright red scarf.

Maria Kharchevna closed the door of the classroom. As she greeted the students and welcomed them to the new school year, her eyes seemed to linger on Ivan's bare collar. Her smile dimmed slightly as she raised her eyes from Ivan's collar to his face.

'Before we begin our first lesson, I have an announcement to make that concerns a comrade in our class.' She took a deep breath. 'Our school and, of course, our class have been honoured in that one of us has won the All-Moscow history prize.' Ivan felt his cheeks become hot. 'We are most pleased that in this way, our glorious leader, Comrade Lenin, also has been honoured.' The teacher clapped politely. The class also clapped, some of the students looking from side to side to see who had won the prize. Maria Kharchevna continued. 'The winner of this prize is Ivan Nazaroff – if you will please stand one moment, Ivan.'

Ivan stood beside his desk. The class stared at him. Many of the children were classmates from the year before. They knew why Ivan did not wear the red scarf. Others looked at him curiously. Ivan could feel his heart pounding beneath his shirt. 'The honour is for You, Lord Jesus,' he said silently, smiling shyly at his class.

'Thank you, Comrade. You may sit down.' The teacher took her place beside the square blackboard. 'We will begin our first day with a review of mathematics. I trust you have not forgotten everything over the summer vacation.'

Ivan opened his book and looked at the page. The

numbers swam in front of his eyes. The teacher had said nothing about the trip to America. Could it mean that he would not be permitted to go?

It was difficult for Ivan to concentrate on his schoolwork. Even the first history lesson, his favorite subject, seemed boring. It too was a review. Once again, the teacher told how the Soviet Union had triumphed over all its enemies in the Glorious Revolution. Only the Great Patriotic War had temporarily set back the progress of the Soviet Union. The children must never forget the heroism

of the Soviet army and Soviet people which was known throughout the world.

Ivan had heard these words many times. But today as the phrase 'throughout the world' fell on his ears, he felt a thrill of excitement. Perhaps he would soon see a part of that world outside the Soviet Union. He looked up with glowing eyes at Maria Kharchevna. Seeing his excitement, she misunderstood and smiled briefly at his enthusiasm for the heroism of the Soviet army.

Finally, the end of the school day arrived and Ivan presented himself at his new teacher's desk. She motioned for him to sit down in a front row seat, and when the room was entirely emptied of students, she leaned toward him from behind her desk.

'Again, Comrade Nazaroff, I congratulate you on bringing an All-Moscow prize to our school.'

Ivan knew he ought to mention that he had done it for the glory of Soviet youth and the approval of Comrade Lenin. Simply to say 'thank you' would seem to bring attention to himself. Unsure of what to say, he said nothing.

Maria Kharchevna sighed quietly and took a deep breath. 'No doubt you have been informed by letter than the prizewinners will spend five weeks at a foreign school.' Ivan nodded, trying to control his excitement. 'I have reviewed your school records and note that you have studied both English and French. If you did not know English, of course, you would not be able to go.'

The teacher paused and looked hopefully at Ivan.

'Perhaps you feel your English is not advanced enough to study in this difficult language. You can, by all means, decide to wait until your English is at a higher level.'

Ivan answered carefully. 'Of course, Comrade Kharchevna, I would like my English to be perfect before taking such a journey. Although I still make mistakes in the language, I have successfully passed, with not a low grade, conversational English.'

'I am aware of that,' Maria Kharchevna nodded. A look troubled her eyes. 'Even though you are not yet a Young Pioneer, you will be permitted to go. Of course, I would be very pleased if you would join the Young Pioneers at this time. You must agree that you have a very great responsibility to uphold the honour of our glorious country.' She waited for Ivan to answer.

He could feel his heart pounding. 'I do agree, Comrade Kharchevna, that I have a great responsibility. And I will do all that I can to uphold the honour of our school and our country. But, as you know, I am a believer. I cannot also be a Young Pioneer.'

The teacher pressed her lips together before speaking. After a long sigh, she shook her head in disapproval.

'It is my responsibility to encourage you to become a Young Pioneer. I regret you answered as you did. You will be the only student going to America who is not a Young Pioneer.'

Ivan couldn't repress a delighted grin.

27

'Then I really am to go to America? I will be permitted to go?'

Maria Kharchevna drew herself up a little straighter in her chair. 'Certainly you will be able to go. And why not? You won the prize. It is not so unusual for there to be an exchange of students between the Soviet Union and another country! It is not so unusual, is it?'

In all his life, Ivan had never heard of any student being allowed to leave the Soviet Union for a visit to a Western country. He knew some people who disagreed with the government were exiled, never to return. But those who went to the West never came back.

'It is certainly not unusual,' the teacher declared again. Getting up from behind her desk, she sat down next to Ivan. 'You parents are pleased, I am sure.'

'Oh, yes, Comrade Teacher.'

'You would not want to do or say anything on your trip that would cause your parents any embarrassment. You would not want to be the cause of anything difficult for them to explain. You do not look like the kind of boy who would ever hurt your parents in any way, at their jobs, or, well, with the authorities.'

Suddenly Ivan felt very heavy. He glanced at the classroom window which one of the students had closed after the final bell had rung. The window was smeared with dust and rain. Ivan longed to be outside, in autumn wind and fresh air. He took a deep breath and smelled the chalk and staleness of the room.

'No, Comrade Teacher. I will be careful not to bring any trouble to my parents.'

The teacher smoothed back a wisp of blonde hair that fell on her forehead and smiled brightly at Ivan. 'After school tomorrow, you will meet with officials from the committee who will explain the exchange program to you. Do you have any questions?'

Ivan shook his head. He felt as if he might smother in the still air of the classroom.

'Then you may go. And, of course, congratulations again.' The teacher's voice was cool and controlled, her smile slightly stiff.

Walking as quickly as he dared, Ivan hurried through the empty halls and pushed open the heavy door of his school. A gust of wind blew in his face and Ivan took a deep gulp of the air. Suddenly he felt light enough to fly. As soon as he left the grounds of the school, he began to run, buoyed up by a joy that even Maria Kharchevna could not take away.

# The Reception

The days of preparation flew by in a blur of activities. The most lavish event was a reception for the ten prizewinners at a young Pioneer palace in central Moscow. It was a familiar place to the other prizewinners; Young Pioneer palaces around the city were centres of after-school activities for hundreds of thousands of children. Each palace was an impressive building with a gymnasium, hobby and craft rooms, music and dance studios, and playrooms for the youngest of the Pioneers. Many, like this one, had huge meeting rooms that could be used for recitals and receptions.

Ivan looked around the reception hall with open curiosity. As a Christian non-member of Young Pioneers, he had never before been inside a Pioneer palace. Huge chandeliers hung from the ceiling in a long row of blazing light. Massive uncurtained windows reached from the polished wood floor to the ceiling, reflecting the candlelit tables and the people passing back and forth in front of them. The parents of the prizewinners had been given places of honour, guided to a special circle of ornate chairs by a high government official.

The main speaker, an official from the Ministry of Education, was a heavy set man with two chins. He spoke for a long time about the new era of 'openness' between the Soviet Union and the United States. From time to time he became excited in his talk and wagged a plump finger energetically at his audience. Ivan noticed that, when he did this, his whole body shook a little, especially his flabby chins. Ivan smiled slightly, thinking how Katya would have to suppress a giggle if she were present.

After the speech the guests were invited to the tables laden with special food. The serving trays were of polished silver and sparkled under the light of the beautiful chandeliers. There were silver bowls of caviar, plates of green onions and pickled mushrooms, delicate white fish in lemon sauce, chicken salad in sour cream, baskets of special breads, little cakes, and apple sauce with raspberry topping. During the meal lively violin music was played by two Young

Pioneers dressed in the formal uniform of the youth organization.

'We are so proud of you, Ivan!' Momma whispered and squeezed his arm as they selected food for their plates. Over his shoulder Ivan could see Poppa talking to another father. Poppa was good at making friends. Ivan remembered Poppa's prayer that morning that the Lord would give him an opportunity to talk about his faith. He nudged Momma to glance over at Poppa. Momma smiled at the sight of her husband in such deep conversation.

'Even though our country is officially atheistic,' Poppa was fond of saying, his smile crinkling the corners of his eyes, 'in everyone's heart of hearts, there are questions. God has made us to love Him. Only He can fill that empty place in people's hearts.'

Momma nodded happily but spoke to Ivan in a low voice so that no one would overhear. 'We still do not begin such conversations, Ivan. Even now, we must be careful not to anger or offend our comrades. But often – very often, it seems – people ask questions of us that we can answer by sharing a little of our faith.'

After their plates were full, Momma nudged Ivan in the direction of Poppa. Balancing the plates so the food would not spill, they approached the two fathers.

Momma smiled in greeting, her cheeks slightly pink from the excitement of the evening. She offered her plate to the stranger.

'Please, you men are so busy talking, my son and I have brought you refreshment.' Ivan handed the plate in his hands to Poppa.

The stranger smiled back in appreciation. 'But the line at the table is so long. You will have to wait again.' Momma shrugged as if to indicate it was no trouble at all.

When Ivan finally sat down to his meal, his stomach was rumbling in pleasurable anticipation. Never had he eaten such a luxurious meal. He tried not to think about how soon he would be leaving for America. When he did, the excitement made it hard to swallow.

Later that night, lying on his bed in his small room off the living room, Ivan could not sleep. So much was happening so quickly it was hard to believe it was true. The morning would begin a whole week of special meetings for the prizewinners. They would learn much about America and American customs.

The days after the reception were completely filled with preparation for the American journey. The students were drilled to remember that they were representing the Soviet Union. In talking about their country, they were to admit that the USSR was not perfect. An instructor taught them the questions and criticisms they were likely to encounter and how to handle such situations. Sometimes they broke up into groups of two: one student would pretend to be the American asking questions about the Soviet Union, the other student rehearsing how to answer.

Two teachers would accompany the group as chaperones. Ivan knew these teachers would either be KGB agents or in the pay of the KGB. It would be their responsibility to make sure none of the young people said or did anything that would cause any embarrassment to the government. They would be required to make detailed reports on each student and each student's activities. It was a procedure with

which any active, known Christian in the USSR was familiar.

The woman teacher was Olga Drobovna, a tall, middle-aged woman with an easy smile and dimpled chin. Her glossy dark hair was braided neatly and pinned in a shining coil at the back of her neck. Ivan noticed that her dress was a lovely color of blue, nicer than most of the dresses he had ever seen.

The man teacher was short and dark. He was dressed in a regular Russian suit. He appeared more excited and nervous than Olga Drobovna. Ivan guessed that he had not been to the West before. His name was Yuri Fedorchuk. Of the two, Ivan thought Fedorchuk would be the one to be wary of. Since he was new, he might be eager to report any small rule that might be forgotten. Ivan warned himself to steer clear of Yuri Fedorchuk!

Finally the day of departure came in a rush of activities. Katya's eyes had brimmed with tears when she said goodbye, even though she laughed at herself and hugged Ivan fiercely. Momma had looked a little anxious at the airport and Poppa had prayed and waved his arm in wide half-circles as Ivan disappeared down the ramp to the air plane.

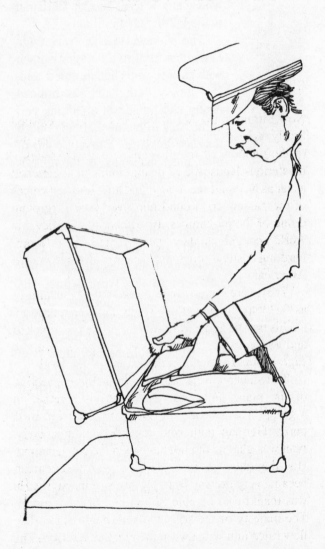

# Journey to the West

Now, sitting in the Aeroflot jet, his seat belt clasped firmly across his lap, Ivan gazed for hours out of the window of the plane as it soared through a mysterious landscape of dense clouds that stretched as far as he could see. Ivan could hear muffled voices of the passengers around him over the background drone of the jet engines. It seemed an unbelievable world, caught as they were in a narrow 'room' hurdling cosily through the expanses of space toward America.

They were served a meal much smaller, but almost as fancy as the one at the Young Pioneer reception. On his tray he had a fresh salad, a white roll, chicken and two cooked vegetables, tea and cake. Ivan ate eagerly, amazed again at the variety of the food.

The students were scattered throughout a section of the plane and were unable to sit together in a group. The seat next to Ivan was occupied by a portly German man who fell asleep immediately. Ivan was glad he did not have to make conversation. His thoughts, at first jumbled with excitement, became very drowsy from the hours of inactivity. He was thankful to be able to look out of the window. The majesty of the still clouds through which they flew filled him with awe at the greatness of God. The unseen earth below him seemed immense. He felt oddly alone and insignificant.

'Young comrade, wake up! Surely you want some breakfast.' The Aeroflot attendant was shaking his shoulder gently. Ivan opened his eyes in confusion. How long had he been asleep? The hum of the plane and the quiet voices around him flooded into his consciousness.

'Breakfast! Oh, yes, if you please,' he answered thickly.

His rotund seat mate smiled and spoke to him in German.

Ivan shrugged foolishly to indicate he did not understand. 'Do you speak English?' he asked, forming the words a little shyly.

'Nein.' It was the German's turn to shrug helplessly. They exchanged a smile as the breakfast trays were placed onto the seat trays in front of them.

Outside the plane the sky had turned from black to grey. Gentle pink and orange colors glowed across the edge of the clouds. Ivan sipped his scalding tea gratefully and tried to calm himself. His heart was pounding with excitement.

'Good morning, comrades, ladies and gentlemen,' the captain's voice cut into Ivan's thoughts. 'We will be landing at Kennedy Airport in New York in about one hour. The weather in New York is very good: sunny and mild. The temperature at the moment is sixty-five degrees. The time in New York is now seven a.m. Enjoy your breakfast.'

The German who had eased himself out of his seat to stretch his legs began walking down the long aisle of the plane. Olga Drobovna appeared and slid into the empty seat. She gave Ivan an understanding smile. 'Well, comrade, are you excited?'

Ivan was glad to see her familiar face. 'Yes!'

'When we get off the plane, make sure you have everything with you.'

Ivan nodded.

'We are all meeting just at the entrance to the terminal, after we get off the plane. Then we will go together through the passport control. In case there are any problems, Comrade Fedorchuk and I will be able to help.'

Ivan nodded again, wishing he could think of something to say. He felt he might explode with excitement. The teacher smiled briefly and was gone. Ivan turned again to the window. The sky was blazing with bright color. 'Thank You, Lord, that You are with me,' he breathed. 'Help me to be a good witness for You in America! Help me to do well at the school. Be with Momma and Poppa and Katya.'

Ivan grinned as he remembered Katya's farewell. Still smiling through her tears she had given him a prized possession, a beautiful little antique silver spoon, the handle inset with a dark blue glaze and decorated with delicate silver intertwining circles. It had been a New Year's gift for Katya when she was a baby.

'Perhaps you will want a present for someone you will meet,' Katya had said. 'Take it for me, Ivan, so I'll feel in a little way as if I too am going.'

'I'll carry it in my pocket everywhere I go,' Ivan had promised. When he had looked up, the tears were slipping down Katya's cheeks. 'I'll miss you so much, Ivan. I'll pray for you so much.'

His thoughts were interrupted by the sharp descent of the plane. Ivan strained to see as much as he could. The sun turned the deep blue coastal waters to a blinding silver. Suddenly they were over land and Ivan was able to see the towering sky-scrapers of New York City.

In a matter of minutes, the jet skimmed across the airport runway and slowed to a graceful stop. Ivan was in America.

# Welcome to America

Color blazed from every surface in the New York air terminal! It was as if all of life's colors at home were soft browns and greys. Here bright reds and blues and silver streaked across the walls on posters and signs. English words seemed to leap out at Ivan in bold lettering. The terminal was lit brilliantly and neon lights flashed over little shops and restaurants. Everywhere there were things to buy and everything looked clean and new.

The prizewinning Moscow students had felt privileged and important in Moscow. Now, hurrying through the New York terminal, they felt unexpectedly foreign. For reasons they did not understand, they stood out. People glanced at them, their eyes holding just a moment longer than usual on the small group. Ivan tried to suppress a smile that wouldn't be subdued. Here Christians were not despised! He searched every face for a clue, looking for other Christians.

'We will meet the American teacher at the baggage area.' Comrade Drobovna's heels tapped confidently across the shiny floor.

'Welcome! Welcome to the United States!' The group slowed down and stopped at the greeting. 'Are you Miss Drobovna?' The American consulted a small paper he held in his hand. He was a tall man of about thirty with brown hair and brown-rimmed glasses. He wore blue jeans, a fact which all of the students noticed immediately. Smiling broadly, he shook hands with both teachers and then turned to the group of students. 'It's a great pleasure to welcome each of you to America. I'm David Bradley from Stephen Academy.'

Ivan marvelled at the goodwill of Mr. Bradley. For the next few minutes he energetically pulled the suitcases indicated by the teachers and students off the conveyor belt. When anyone tried to help him, he waved them away saying they were tired after a long flight. Piling the luggage on a large trolley, he made his way to the exit and into the parking lot and the morning sunshine.

Ivan walked beside Lida Ligachovna, the prizewinner in physics. She was a girl with a round cheerful face and curly black hair. 'I can hardly believe this is true!' she whispered to Ivan, shifting her carry-on case from hand to hand. 'Everything is so fast and different!'

Mr. Bradley stopped beside a huge white van. He slid the door of the van open and motioned for the students to get in. The teachers sat in the front with him, chatting politely as they weaved their way through the morning traffic and onto the main road. The streets were jammed with rush-hour traffic.

'What a lot of automobiles!' Vladimir Potopov remarked. He was the biology winner and was concerned about the pollution.

Mr. Bradley laughed easily. 'Yes, too many, I'd say! Traffic in New York City seems to get worse every year. But all this will thin out once we get outside the city.'

Soon they were driving east through beautiful countryside. As far as they could see, rolling hills stretched into the horizon. From time to time they passed over stone-arched bridges. In deep ravines beneath the bridges, sparkling blue streams spilled over tumbles of rocks. Herds of cattle grazed peacefully in the distance. It looked so unspoiled and lovely it reminded Ivan of Poppa's descriptions of the Old Testament promised land of milk and honey. All the young people were fascinated with their first view of America, none more than Ivan and Vladimir Potopov, the biology winner. Vladimir gazed raptly at the trees and meadows and pasture lands, exclaiming softly from time to time when he saw some tree or bush he could identify.

Mr. Bradley kept up a steady flow of friendly chatter, pointing out any facts of interest that came to his mind. When they crossed the border from New York state to Vermont, where Stephen Academy was located, he pointed out the sign that said, 'Welcome to Vermont.' North of Vermont, he told them, was the Canadian province of Quebec. Vermont, as well as Quebec, was famous for its maple syrup, for the ski lodges in the Green Mountains and for dairy farming.

It didn't seem long before they were seeing signs to Stephen Academy. Soon Mr. Bradley slowed the van to pass through a formal red-brick gate, along a narrow tree-lined road that widened into a circular drive in front of the school. Everyone, even Olga Drobovna and Yuri Fedorchuk, twisted in their seats or leaned around someone else to get a first glimpse of the place where they would be spending the next five weeks. It was a fine red-brick building built on a low hill. Gardens blazing with autumn flowers of orange and red circled the driveway.

Mr. Bradley brought the van to a stop at the bottom of a low flight of brick steps that led up to the school's graceful veranda. 'Welcome to Stephen's Academy!' he said with a flourish of his voice. He jumped out and slid open the door on the wide side of the van. 'Everybody out!

'This is the main school building – classrooms and offices.' He turned toward the imposing ivy-covered structure beyond the van. Through the trees the group could see other buildings. Following their gazes, Mr. Bradley identified the student dormitories. On the other side of the circular drive on higher ground than the school was a small brick building nestled in a few trees and well-trimmed bushes. 'That is our chapel,' Mr. Bradley said quietly. Ivan stared at the lovely little building with the wide white door. He thought of Russia in the ancient times of the czars when very different small chapels were built for the royal family and court beside all their summer homes. Even in the Kremlin itself, in Moscow's Red Square, Czar Ivan the Terrible had ordered seven wooden chapels built that were later rebuilt in stone to become the magnificent St. Basil's Cathedral.

Olga Drobovna tugged on Ivan's arm. 'Are you falling asleep, Ivan? Come. We are going inside to meet the headmaster and some students. Soon you will all be able to rest for a little while.'

The headmaster was silver-haired and athletic-looking. He strode out of his office and down the hall with a wide smile of greeting to meet the group as they entered the building. 'It is a great pleasure to welcome you all to America and also to Stephen Academy!' One by one, he went to each member of the group, starting with the teachers and passing from one student to the next with a warm handshake. Chairs had been set up in his spacious office and he waved the group toward them. 'You have had a very long journey, flying direct from Moscow to New York. I know you need rest. Mr. Bradley will be taking you to your rooms right away,' he smiled understandingly at the group, 'but I want you to know that we are delighted to have you with us. After you have rested, we have planned a little reception for you.'

Later, Ivan was to remember the first hours at Stephen as a blur of smiles and greetings. He felt groggy after a brief nap. He tried to nibble the small American sandwiches laid out on a white cloth. A buzz of unfamiliar American-accented English floated around him. About a dozen American students, the boys dressed in jackets and shirts and ties, the girls in dresses, greeted them and made conversation. Ivan was aware that Olga Drobovna and Yuri Fedorchuk circulated in the group, listening to the conversations. One American girl hung back. Mr. Bradley noticed her on the edge of the circle and brought her over to Ivan. 'Ivan, I'd like you to meet Courtney Campbell.'

She had long, straight blond hair that hung halfway down her back and the bluest eyes Ivan could ever remember seeing. They were icy blue, unwarmed by the polite smile she gave Ivan. 'I'm pleased to meet someone from Vermont,' Ivan smiled.

Courtney's expression remained unchanged. 'I'm sorry,' she said, lifting her chin slightly. 'I am from California. Do you know where that is?'

'California is on the West Coast of the United States, I believe,' Ivan began. 'It is the third largest of your states and the centre for producing television films and motion pictures. It also has a very favorable climate, does it not?'

Courtney looked unimpressed. 'You memorise well.' With that, she turned and walked away deliberately, her long golden hair swinging as she went.

Something was wrong, but Ivan didn't know what.

# Whisper in the Night

When Ivan awoke, it was pitch dark in his room. A slender shaft of moonlight struck the floor in a silver pool of light. For several minutes he struggled to remember where he was. A strange silence wrapped the room in mystery. No Moscow traffic came faintly to his ears. No occasional distant banging could be heard from another part of the apartment building.

Ivan raised himself in bed. Across the wide room, his roommate, Josif Lamekin, slept soundly. With a thrill of excitement, Ivan remembered: they were in America! He swung himself slowly out of bed and for a few minutes he stood at the window, gazing at the moonlit hills sloping off into the distance.

Quietly, Ivan opened the bedroom door and made his way to the lounge at the end of the hall. The carpet was thick under his bare feet. He sank into a deep sofa at one end of the room and stretched both arms across the sofa back, enjoying the feeling of having such a room to himself. The room extended all the way across the west side of the building, with chairs and sofas arranged, hotel-like, in small groupings.

Without the silence being broken in any way that Ivan could hear, he knew that someone had entered the room. His heart pounded wildly. 'What if it isn't permitted to come into this room at night?' Ivan shrank back into the cushions listening so intently that he could make out faint movement somewhere in the room. Then he heard a metallic click followed immediately by eleven careful, quieter clicks.

After a moment a low voice in Russian-accented English whispered, 'I am a Russian student. I wish to defect. I will call back when the office is open.' Ivan recognized the sound of a telephone receiver being replaced. Holding his breath in shock, he strained to see even the outline of the person who had made such a call. No form crossed the splash of moonlight on the floor. After remaining frozen in position for a long time, Ivan relaxed his body and stood up cautiously. The whole dormitory seemed sound asleep. But Ivan knew, somewhere in the building, one of his comrades was lying in the dark, with a heart pounding as fearfully as his own.

By morning, Ivan had had time to think about the seriousness of what he had heard. If someone in the group were to defect to America, it could go badly for the whole group. Everyone would be suspect as accomplices. The exchange program itself might be endangered. Perhaps they would all be returned to the Soviet Union without ever having the chance to study in America. Worse than all that, if the plan were discovered the one attempting to defect would most certainly be punished on return to the Soviet Union.

Ivan moved along at the end of the Saturday morning breakfast line, surprised at the large selection of food that was laid out for the students of the academy. He was also amazed at the loud buzz of conversation in the room: American students were talking and laughing together as they ate. Anyone could overhear them, but they seemed unconcerned. In a Russian school, the dining room would have been quiet, the students eating silently and then leaving.

Ivan chose orange juice and tea, bread and butter and jam, an egg and sausages and a white roll. He was the last person in the group to join the special table reserved for the Russian students. Quietly, he bowed his head and thanked God for the wonderful food and the new day. When he raised his eyes, he noticed a flush of disapproval on the faces of the Russian teachers.

Ivan glanced around the table, trying to guess who might have made the secret call. Everyone looked innocent and rested, eating silently and quickly. Seated next to Ivan, the oldest student in the group, Michael Semedi, winner of the mathematics prize, was cutting his bread into perfect squares and buttering them, one by one. Lida, her round cheeks scrubbed pink, her curls flattened by two barrettes, was shyly watching the Americans at the next table. As Ivan ate, he glanced around the table at each member of the group: Vladimir, Josif, Luba, Alexi, Georgi, Yuri and Irina. None of them looked the least bit nervous or secretive. It almost seemed as if the telephone call in the middle of the night never happened.

As his eyes shifted from one student to another,

Ivan caught the searching glance of Comrade Drobovna. She put down her tea-cup and leaned toward Ivan. 'You look worried this morning, Ivan. Is something wrong?'

The questions was so unexpected Ivan choked on his orange juice. 'Oh no!' he gasped when he could speak. 'Excuse me, comrade. I choked on my juice.'

'So I see,' she answered quietly. She gazed thoughtfully at Ivan and then turned to Comrade Fedorchuk with a friendly comment.

Ivan felt a pang of guilt. He tried to calm himself. 'All I did was sit in the lounge,' he reminded himself. 'That's nothing to feel so guilty about.' But the whispered words he had overheard had burned themselves into his mind.

The morning was spent in touring the grounds of the school, visiting the well-equipped gymnasium, the football and soccer fields, classrooms, labs and the assembly hall. As they moved from building to building, Ivan noticed how generously telephones were scattered around the campus. Almost every room had a telephone. Once or twice Ivan thought he caught the glance of one of the chaperones observing his interest in the telephones. He looked away quickly. When the students were shown around the lounge, Ivan saw the telephone that had been used in the middle of the night. It was on a side table in a corner of the room.

At eleven o'clock they were to have tea with the Vermont education official who had helped arrange the students' exchange program. She was a tall grey-haired woman. Her smile was warm and reserved.

'We are extremely pleased to welcome you young people to the United States. We requested winners of a contest that would represent a cross-section of Soviet young people. You are different ages and different sexes, of course. You are all from different specialities of learning: mathematics, biology, history, physics and so on. Some of you have parents who are factory workers and some of your parents work for the government. At least one of you represents one of the religious groups in the Soviet Union.' Ivan flushed. So that was why a believer had been allowed to enter the contest! The calm voice of the woman continued. 'And the fact that you are finally here is a sign of the new openness that your leader, Mr. Gorbachev, has promised is beginning. Your five weeks in this country will go fast. Before you know it, it will be time for you to return home. I know you will make the most of your opportunity. Welcome!'

Ivan applauded politely with the rest of the group. The smile on his face hid the sinking thought that struck him: One of us is planning that in five weeks he or she will not return to our country!

# The Man in the Grey Suit

It was a quiet Saturday evening after a long, full day. There had been the school tour in the morning and the greeting by the education official. In the afternoon, they had all attended a football game in a small stadium in a nearby town. The Stephen Academy team was playing a rival school.

Ivan had loved the American football game. Among the Moscow prize-winners, Ivan was the only athlete. 'I want to introduce you to the team.' Mr. Bradley had pulled Ivan down from the stands to the Stephen team bench at half-time. Stephen Academy was winning by two touchdowns. The coach and the team, proud in their red and white uniforms, greeted Ivan warmly. The coach invited Ivan to sit on the bench and watch the game from the sidelines.

American students, Ivan observed, were full of open laughter and energy – running up and down the stands, calling to their friends, waving, eating; it seemed to him that there was almost as much activity in the stands as on the field. All the same, everyone followed the game intently, cheering the teams on. When the last whistle blew and the game was over, the Stephen Academy stands erupted in an explosion of celebration.

As Ivan stood in the golden sunlight of the late afternoon, with movement all around him, his eyes were drawn to a man in a grey business suit standing alone at the edge of the stands. He was staring up at the group of Russian students as if he were looking for someone. As the group made its way toward the exit, the man backed slowly into the crowd, taking one last searching look at the group. Ivan hurriedly extended his hand to the coach.

'Thank you for letting me sit with the team. It was very exciting to be here.' The coach was surrounded by several of the jubilant players. They too shook Ivan's hand vigorously.

'I see our group is leaving. I have to hurry.' Ivan hoped he wasn't being rude.

'Of course. Come and watch us at practice any time. Hope you enjoy your time at Stephen Academy!' Ivan nodded while trying to keep the man in his view as long as he could. Comrade Fedorchuk was waiting for Ivan, motioning slightly to let Ivan know he needed to hurry. Ivan jogged toward the group, looking over his shoulder for the man in the grey business suit. He had disappeared.

Now, in the peace of the New England evening, sitting on a quiet bench under a spreading tree, Ivan relaxed in the summer air. There were a few minutes before the group was to have a meeting. Ivan's thoughts were in turmoil. Something strange was going on and he had a foreboding of trouble.

A girl coming across campus caught his attention. Ivan lazily watched her, thinking how differently

American girls walked: they swung their arms more than girls at home and took longer steps. The girl had long blond hair.

'Hi, Ivan.' Courtney sat down on the edge of the end of Ivan's bench managing a thin smile.

'Hello, Courtney Campbell. Hello. How are you?' Ivan had stood up when she appeared and now sat down, a little uncertain of what to do.

'I came over to find out if you want to go to church in the morning.'

'Oh, yes! I would like that very much! Is it all right?'

'Well, of course. If you want to come.'

'But, Courtney Campbell – I mean, I do not wish to inconvenience you. And, of course, I have to get permission.'

'Really?' The girl smoothed a long lock of her heavy blond hair.

'Well, I'm sure it's all right to go, but I have to ask one of our teachers.'

The girl laughed. 'I don't think you need permission just to go to church.'

'All the same…' Ivan smiled a little at the girl, not sure of how to ask the question. 'Are you…?' He stopped and took a deep breath and did not speak again.

'Am I what?'

'You know, a believer.'

'Saved?'

'Yes.'

'Since I was four.'

Ivan dropped his voice. 'I too am a believer.'

Courtney gave Ivan a polite smile. 'I know. Mr. Bradley told me you were the Christian in the group. He wants to know if you want to go to church tomorrow morning.'

Ivan stared. 'You knew?'

'Of course! You don't think I would walk up to just anybody and ask them if they want to go to church, do you?'

'Certainly I think you would, Courtney Campbell. This is America! No one will report you or fine you or follow you if you ask someone such a thing!'

The girl looked at Ivan strangely and after a moment stood up. 'Mr. Bradley will take us at 9:30.'

Ivan nodded.

'And don't call me Courtney Campbell all the time! My first name is enough!' she called back with a toss of her head.

Ivan stood for a second thinking about how irritated Courtney had seemed. With a shrug, he hurried inside the administration building to the first floor lounge where the meeting was to begin.

The teachers explained what they had seen that day, pointing out features of American culture and education that arose from their experiences. As the time wore on, Ivan felt drowsy. He struggled to stay awake, and against his will his eyes closed for a moment. Into the fog of his tiredness came a whisper. For a few seconds, Ivan listened drowsily to the whispering and then bolted awake. He was certain it was the same low voice he had heard the night before in the lounge!

Turning his head slowly, Ivan glanced at the row behind him. Georgi Koragin returned Ivan's startled look with a reproving glance. 'Stay awake, comrade!' Next to Georgi, Yuri Fedorov had stretched out his legs under Ivan's chair. As Ivan turned, the chair shifted slightly and wrenched his legs. Yuri gave Ivan an irritated look and withdrew his legs. On the other side of Georgi, Lida Ligachovna sat with folded hands. She smiled at Ivan, turning to Georgi and Yuri with a pretty frown before returning her attention to the lecture at the front of the chairs.

Before long they were making their way back to their rooms in the dormitories. Ivan walked along, trying to greet or speak a word or two to everyone in the group. No one appeared nervous or upset. They were all chatting quietly or walking alone, tired from the experiences of the day.

'Perhaps I dreamed the call in the middle of the night. Perhaps I didn't hear anyone whisper.' Ivan tossed on his soft American bed, getting his feet tangled in the sheet.

'Lord Jesus, help me to be wise and to know what is right. If someone is trying to defect, show me what is right to do.' Ivan fell into a fitful sleep. When he awoke, it was already morning and Josif was shaking him to get ready for breakfast. Whatever might have happened in the night, Ivan had missed it.

# An American Church

Ivan was not surprised that Comrade Drobovna decided to accompany him to church. He knew that one of her jobs was to keep daily reports on the students. If Ivan were to be away from the group for several hours, who would know what he did or what he might have said?

Courtney was waiting for him in front of the school. Her hair was pulled back tightly and held in a long green-ribboned braid. She looked fresh and pretty as she tucked herself into the back seat of the van. Mr. Bradley greeted Olga Drobovna with a cheerful smile, as if it were the most natural thing in the world that a member of the Communist Party of Moscow would visit a small New England church.

'This will be an interesting cultural experience,' Olga Drobovna said. 'In the Soviet Union, although we are, of course, an atheistic state, there are still some of our older citizens who go to prayer houses. And, of course, they are perfectly free to do so. I myself, naturally, have never been inside these prayer houses.'

Ivan gazed out of the window at the rising hills and said nothing.

'How many Christians would you say there are in the Soviet Union?' Mr. Bradley asked.

Olga Drobovna shrugged. 'Oh, very few. Out of a people of 280 million, there are very few.'

Ivan's face burned with indignation at Comrade Drobovna's untruthful words. He tried to joke. 'Well, of course, I am one of them.'

Courtney's cool blue eyes glanced at Ivan with a shade of suspicion. 'I heard there is no freedom for Christians in Russia. That sometimes they are sent to labour camps or are fined or have to suffer in lots of ways.'

Ivan's mouth went dry and his mind a blank. How could he explain it all to Courtney? The group had been told they must not say anything negative about their mother country. He was bursting to tell Courtney about his own friend, Pyotr, who was once taken away from his mother and put in a state school because his mother persisted in

teaching him about God.[1] He wanted to tell Courtney about pastors who had been sent to labour camps because they were too active in their churches. And about informers in the church and the shortage of

1. Read this story in *Ivan and the Daring Escape*

Bibles and how uncertain the church situation was, even in this new era of glasnost!

Olga Drobovna's light laughter broke the silence that followed Courtney's question. 'I think Ivan here is experiencing our Soviet freedom to the full and enjoying it, too. Aren't you enjoying it, Ivan?'

'Yes.' Ivan knew his voice was strained and that Comrade Drobovna would be displeased that he had not answered Courtney directly with the official Soviet response. It was true, Ivan would have admitted, that Soviet law allowed a church service on Sundays for adults. But Comrade Drobovna made the situation sound much better than it really was.

Mr. Bradley slowed the van as they entered a nearby village with broad, winding streets. He pulled into a small parking lot to the side of a white frame church. In spite of his confusion in the van, Ivan's spirits rose as he saw people going into the church. Everything was open and public. People were not hurrying to enter the church so they could not be seen. Some were chatting on the church steps. People greeted each other and lingered in the bright sunlight. Almost everyone carried a Bible. Ivan was amazed. He tried not to stare although his eyes went again and again to the precious book.

Later, Ivan wondered what effect the church service had on Olga Drobovna. But as soon as he entered the church he forgot about her. He was overwhelmed by beauty. The floors and pews gleamed as if they had been newly polished. The windows were high and wide, bordered by white wood. He could see the branches of leafy trees outside framed by the lovely windows. The pulpit jutted out from the side of the platform. The whole sanctuary was open and full of light.

Ivan supposed they were early. Less than half the church was filled. At the front were several empty rows of pews. People were sitting in little clusters of twos and threes, whispering from time to time as an unseen organ played softly. Emotions of love and happiness flooded Ivan. He felt deeply at home.

Ivan thought of his own crowded church in Moscow on a side street of the busy city. There were never enough seats for everyone in spite of the fact that people pushed together in the pews to make as much room as possible. People without seats stood along the walls of the sanctuary, thankful to be part of the worship even if they could not sit down. Many would have stood willingly outside on the street by the windows just to hear the singing and the preaching but the pastors could not allow it. Many believers were turned away every Sunday and had to return home without even getting inside the church building.

The singing in America was very different. At the first hymn, Ivan sang loudly, his voice full of the joy he felt. Courtney turned pointedly to him and widened her unsmiling eyes. Ivan blushed in embarrassment as he heard his own voice booming above the faint singing.

There were Bibles in the pew rack. When the Scripture was announced, Ivan lifted out a Bible with a shaking hand. Without opening it, he held it in both hands, running his thumb across the black cover. He felt alarmed that so many Bibles were left scattered in the racks throughout the church. Anyone could come into the church and take them! As he opened the Bible reverently, he felt a longing to have a Bible of his own. In Moscow, the idea had been impossible. But perhaps here in America, he could find one to buy!

The pastor preached in a warm, clear voice. The sermon was about Jesus stilling the storms of life. Jesus can protect us. In His presence we are safe. To all our fears and uncertainties He says, 'Peace.'

Tears stung Ivan's eyes. The pastor's words were wonderful. Ivan knew that Momma and Poppa and Katya were safe because they were in Jesus' care. Jesus would be present with the believers in the labour camps, those who were hated because of their Christian faith, those who were afraid that they might not be able to bear the hardships of the Christian life.

It seemed to Ivan that the sermon was finished very quickly. In Moscow, it would have been much longer and several pastors would have preached. People left the church smiling and nodding to one another. A few children broke away from their parents and huddled together whispering and visiting. Ivan noticed some academy students chatting at the back. Courtney slipped out of the end of the pew and waved a general goodbye.

The American pastor stood at the back of the

church, greeting the believers and shaking their hands. He smiled warmly and shook Ivan's hand vigorously when they were introduced. 'We are very glad to have you visit with us. It's not every Sunday we have a believer from Russia worshipping with us!' He grinned at his own joke, and Ivan smiled too. 'Would you consider speaking to our young people sometime while you are here? I know how much they would enjoy it.'

Ivan thought of Courtney's coolness and felt unsure. 'If you would like...' His answer reflected his uncertainty.

'Wonderful!' The pastor smiled at Mr. Bradley and Olga Drobovna, who was looking very dubious. 'Wonderful! I'll telephone you sometime soon to make the arrangements.' Ivan noticed Comrade Drobovna stood a little apart from the minister and did not shake his hand.

'Well, Ivan,' Mr. Bradley was striding in his American way to the van, 'how did you like the church service? Was it very different from your own church in Moscow?'

'I liked it very much!' Ivan stole a glance at Olga Drobovna. She was looking unsettled by the unpredictable morning. 'What the pastor said was a great encouragement to me. It was a very good message from the Lord. I will not forget his words.' Ivan thought it would be best not to attempt a comparison of the two churches with Olga Drobovna's watchful eyes and ears upon him. He was sure to say something that would displease her.

'Courtney is staying in the village to have Sunday dinner with some friends. If you are tired, Ivan, you'll have time for a quick nap before our meal at the academy. It's just a little after eleven now. Our Sunday dinner won't be until twelve-thirty.'

As Mr. Bradley helped Olga Drobovna up into the van, a sudden idea popped into Ivan's head. 'Is it far back to the academy?'

Mr. Bradley grinned. 'I can read your mind. It is about a half-hour walk. Straight down this road.'

'Please may I walk?' Ivan raised his head to Comrade Drobovna with a hopeful lilt in his voice. 'I would very much like the exercise.'

Olga Drobovna forced a dimpled smile so that only her eyes betrayed her concern. Ivan tried not to let even the suggestion of a smile show his amusement. He knew she would not want to let anyone in the group be unsupervised, least of all, him. He suspected that she would not be able to come up with a reason to forbid the walk. He waited to see what she would do.

After a long moment she smiled again. 'Of course, if you wish to walk to the school, you are free to do so. Why not have a walk? Perhaps I should also take some exercise.'

In spite of himself, Ivan looked down in disappointment. He very much wanted to be alone, to walk in this beautiful countryside and to think again of the words the pastor had said.

Mr. Bradley seemed not to have heard Olga Drobovna's last words. Carefully he shut her door and moved around the front of the van to the driver's seat. 'Have a nice walk, Ivan!' he called as he jumped into the van and slammed his door. With a wink to Ivan, he pulled away. As the van disappeared around a turn in the road, Ivan took a deep, happy breath and let the feeling of freedom flow over him.

The Sunday morning was very still. The only sound was Ivan's steps as he strolled along the street.

With one exception, the few stores in the villages seemed to be closed. A sandy-colored dog slept by a gas pump at the corner station just ahead. Ivan picked up his pace and walked briskly along the street, finding the most ordinary things interesting, looking intently at everything as he passed.

At the corner, he paused by the curb to gaze at the American dog. Suddenly he heard a whisper that sent terror into his heart.

# A Secret Plan

Ivan turned sharply in the direction of the whisper. He saw nothing. Confused, he hesitated at the corner. Had he imagined the whisper? It had sounded exactly like the mysterious voice he had heard in the middle of the night. 'Perhaps I am imagining things.' He began walking when he heard it again. It stopped him instantly.

'Ivan! Nazaroff! Over here!'

Just around the corner, pressed against a shop doorway, was Georgi Koragin. Ivan stared in amazement. Georgi's dark hair was matted against his head. His face was white with anxiety.

'Over here!'

Ivan was beside him in two strides. Georgi pulled him into the doorway. 'Nazaroff! I'm in trouble. You've got to help me.'

Georgi's hand clutched Ivan's sleeve and pulled him closer. 'Will you help me?'

Ivan glanced fearfully over his shoulder. The street was still deserted. Across the road was a little park, the entrance flanked by high bushes. 'Let's go into the park.' Ivan pulled away from Georgi's grasp and ran across the empty road.

The boys made for a bench that was away from

the winding footpath and hidden from the road. Georgi's eyes stared intently at Ivan's face. 'You've got to help me.'

In his fear, Ivan called on the Lord for help as they crossed the road. 'Lord, give me wisdom. Help me to know what to do. Help me to help Georgi. Help me not to get Momma and Poppa into trouble.'

'I'll do anything I can, Georgi. Try not to be afraid.'

'You Christians – you're not allowed to report people, are you? You're supposed to help everybody, aren't you? Don't you have to help people?'

Ivan smiled in spite of his anxiety.

'Georgi, we want to help people. Because we know the love of God, we love others. Now tell me what is going on.'

'Do you promise not to report me? If you won't help me, you'll go back and say nothing?'

'But I will help you in any way that I can. You can trust me.'

Georgi looked at a cascading fountain in the centre of the small park. He avoided Ivan's eyes as he spoke. 'When I knew I would be coming to America, I decided to try to stay. My parents are dead and my grandfather understands and wants me to have a new life in the West. Even though I will never see him again, he helped me plan what to do.'

Georgi fell silent with emotion. Struggling for control he went on. 'I tried to call the FBI in New York, but a talking machine told me to leave a message. I started to leave a message but I didn't give my name because I was afraid. Then last night I thought I should write a letter and explain everything and maybe someone from the FBI would come and help me. We have five weeks. I wrote telling about myself and asking for help in defecting to the United States. I wrote it in the night. I didn't think Yuri would see.' Georgi turned and looked helplessly at Ivan.

'Yuri is your roommate?'

Georgi nodded. 'I went to sleep. This morning when I got up, the letter was gone. I hid it in a book on my desk, but it was gone.'

'You think Yuri took it?'

'I am certain of it. Think of how he will be praised for reporting me. I was frightened, Ivan. I didn't know where to go or what to do. I knew you were a Christian and Christians have to help people. I watched for a chance to talk to you alone. I heard you talking with Mr. Bradley about going to the church. After you left, I walked into the village and waited.'

'But you didn't know I would be walking home.' Ivan's heart tightened in fear.

What if this were a trap? What if Georgi were spying on him and setting up a way to get a Christian into trouble?

Georgi nodded. 'I didn't know what else to do. I thought maybe you and the girl would look around the village. Or if nothing else, I was going to try to ask Mr. Bradley to help me. But, of course, Comrade Drobovna came with you. I watched when you came out of the church. I saw her drive away with Mr. Bradley. I saw you walking.'

Ivan took a deep breath. 'Georgi, I heard you make the telephone call in the lounge on Friday night.'

'You did? And you didn't tell?'

'I didn't know who was speaking.' Georgi gave Ivan a terrified look. Ivan added hastily, 'But I wouldn't have told, anyway.'

'What am I going to do? Yuri Fedorchuk or Olga Drobovna must already know. They will be looking for me. I had to run away. I couldn't stay at the academy.'

'Georgi, I don't know what to do either. But if I don't get back right away to the academy, they will be looking for me!'

'Perhaps you would try to telephone the FBI again for me? It is in New York City. They would know what to do. Maybe during the day, even on a Sunday, there is someone to answer the telephone.'

Ivan was thinking as fast as he could. 'You can't come back to Stephen Academy. You will have to stay in town, out of sight, until dark. Then come back to the academy. Do you remember the chapel?'

Georgi nodded.

'Mr. Bradley said it is always open for people to pray. If it is unlocked at night, maybe you could hide in there. Anyway come to the chapel by ten, if you can, and I'll meet you there. They will have already searched the grounds. Nobody will be looking for you on the campus by then. In the meantime, I'll try to think about what I can do.'

A car slowed down at the park and both boys slipped off the bench and crouched in the bushes. Georgi grabbed Ivan's arm in fright. Ivan felt his heart pounding wildly. But the car moved on.

'You stay here. I think there was a little store a couple of blocks back that was open to sell food. I will get you something to eat.'

'I can get it!' Georgi exclaimed. 'You have to get back to the academy!'

'No one must see you in town!' Ivan's voice was sharper than he intended. Taking a slow breath, he continued, 'I can buy something to eat as I walk back to school. This would not be suspicious. I will bring you what I can in a minute.'

Ivan hurried out of the park. The dog by the gas pumps had roused himself and he barked with surprising energy as Ivan passed. Ivan slowed his pace as he came to the little store.

Inside he saw apples in a bin. He picked one up and gazed around the store for something else to buy. An old man wearing braces over a white shirt was sitting behind a wooden counter. Ivan approached him. 'Good afternoon.'

'Yep,' the man answered, looking Ivan up and down.

'Do you have something in a bottle to drink?'

The man continued to gaze at Ivan so long, Ivan thought he might not answer. Finally he said, 'Can.'

'Can?' Ivan couldn't understand. 'Can?'

What could the old man mean?

The man pointed to a refrigerator with a glass door. Inside Ivan could see Pepsi-Cola. Quickly he opened the door and removed the can of soda.

'You new here?' The man had raised himself slowly to his feet.

'I am a visiting student at the academy for five weeks. I am just walking back from church.'

The man nodded.

'Do you have something to eat I could buy?' Ivan was looking at the unfamiliar groceries.

'Cookies. Candy bars.' The man jerked his thumb to a rack standing by the side of the counter. Quickly Ivan pulled a package of cookies off the rack and removed some American money from his pocket.

'Two-thirty-nine.'

Counting out three one-dollar bills, Ivan offered it to the man. He pressed a lever in an old cash register and the drawer flew open. Silently he held out the change to Ivan.

'Thank you, sir. Goodbye.' Ivan made himself walk slowly to the door.

'Yep.' The man sat down again behind the counter.

Georgi was hiding as far under the bushes as he could get. Ivan gave him the apple and cookies and soda. 'This isn't much, but make it last as long as you can. I'll bring you food tonight if I can.'

Georgi's face was lit with hope. 'Thank you, Ivan. I will never be able to thank you enough.'

'Stay out of sight! Try not to worry. I will pray for you!' Ivan hurried out of the park and onto the road.

He walked as quickly as possible back to the school, and prayed hard that, when he arrived, he would not be asked why it had taken him so long.

# Missing

As he neared the school, Ivan could see Olga Drobovna sitting on the front steps, looking down the road. Ivan had jogged until he came in sight of the academy, then he slowed down to a pleasant stroll.

Olga Drobovna walked out to the road to meet him. She smiled brightly but Ivan noticed a forced cheerfulness in her voice.

'Did you have a nice walk?'

'Yes, Comrade Drobovna. And I stopped at a store to buy soda and fruit.'

'You didn't notice Georgi Koragin anywhere, did you?'

Ivan's heart lurched. He took a deep breath. 'Was he also out for a walk?'

The teacher shook her head. 'I don't know where he is. Of course, if he went for a stroll, he ought to have let me or Comrade Fedorchuk know. You all have clear instructions.'

'Our instructions are very clear, comrade. There is no question that we all must let you know if we leave the group.'

'It is not important. Georgi will turn up.' She took one last look around before they entered the building. 'Perhaps he is already back. It is time for the meal.'

Ivan liked the large sunny room in which all the students ate. Sunday dinner was special. There were tablecloths on the tables and the students were dressed in jackets and slacks, or dresses. As Ivan took his place at the table reserved for the Russian students, he noticed the tension in the group. He supposed they had all been questioned about Georgi. Yuri Fedorov sat next to Comrade Fedorchuk. His face was flushed with excitement and importance, but he said nothing.

Ivan's plate was heaped with the delicious American dinner. Never had he seen such meat as the delicate slices of roast beef that had been served to him. Golden butter melted on top of a mound of mashed potatoes. Green beans, corn, hot rolls, salad – it was a feast he tried to enjoy to the full. He was hungry after his walk, but he thought often about Georgi, nibbling his apple and cookies under the bushes in the park.

Ivan longed for Poppa. To be able to talk over this emergency with him, to be guided by his wisdom, what a relief that would be! But how often Poppa had told Ivan and Katya, 'There will be times when you will have to decide on you own what is the right thing to do. Often there will not be time to come home and talk over problems with the family. At such times, you can be sure that the Lord will guide you. Be sure you keep your attention on the Lord, asking for His help. He will never fail.'

A meeting of the group was called after the meal. Ivan took a seat next to Lida Ligachovna. Her round face looked worried and tears rimmed the bottoms of her eyes. Everyone was silent.

'We are very concerned about Georgi Koragin,' Fedorchuk began. 'We are afraid he might have been influenced by anti-Soviet elements while he was in Russia. He has been confused by those who hate our Soviet way of life. He is in danger of making a mistake that he and his family may greatly regret. At the moment we do not know where he is. Each of you individually has been asked about Georgi, and apparently none of you knows anything about this.'

Olga Drobovna passed her hand lightly across her forehead.

Fedorchuk continued. 'It is important for right now that nothing be said to anyone outside our group. Absolutely nothing must be said, no matter what happens. You must not speak to any American – not a student or teacher or anyone else. It is possible that we can locate Georgi before he does something further he will regret. It is possible, of course, that he is merely exploring on his own.'

Ivan had been gazing down at his knees. He glanced at Yuri Fedorov, Georgi's informer. Fedorchuk's lie produced no change of expression. His face was as blank as he could make it.

'If Georgi just went off on his own for a walk, he may have gotten lost. If that is so, someone will help him to get back to the campus. Then, although he has disobeyed, it is not so serious. For this afternoon, we will not have the schedule we planned. I ask you all to stay in your rooms or close by. If you go out for a walk, do not leave the school grounds. Report to me or Comrade Drobovna about what you are doing. And again, say nothing about this to anyone. And, of course, you may watch American television in the lounge. Are there any questions?'

No one spoke. Slowly the group filed out of the room and went their separate ways. 'Ivan, what will happen?' Lida asked in a whisper. 'Where do think Georgi has gone?'

'Don't worry, Lida. Try to enjoy the afternoon. Write a letter home.'

Lida nodded. She gave Ivan a quiet smile and joined Luba Stepanova, her roommate. Ivan could hear Luba exclaim, 'I am so angry! Why did Georgi have to spoil things!'

Ivan went to the lounge and sat down. He picked up a magazine and opened it on his lap. But he did not look at the pages. He concentrated on the questions swirling about in his mind. How could he find out how to telephone the FBI? And if he knew the number, how could he use any telephone without arousing suspicion? And if he was able to telephone, how much money would it cost to call New York City? In all the instructions the students had been given about life in America, how to make a telephone call from a pay telephone had not been included. And most certainly, there had been no guidelines on how to call the FBI!

Ivan thought of the pastor who had preached that morning. If only he could talk to the pastor! But he didn't know his name or where he lived. The only

American he was acquainted with was Courtney Campbell. Although she was a Christian, she was plainly unwilling to be friends. And, of course, she was in the village.

Ivan grew more and more discouraged. He leaned his back against the soft cushions at the back of the couch. His mind swam with shifting images: Georgi's desperate face, the storekeeper who stared at him, the pastor preaching from the pulpit.

He was jolted alert by someone plopping down on the couch beside him. 'Having a nap?' Courtney tipped her chin a little defiantly as she looked at him.

'Hello!' Ivan sat up so quickly a slight smile softened the challenge of Courtney's face.

'You don't have to jump a mile!'

'I was dozing off.'

'So I noticed.' Courtney hesitated. 'How did you like church?'

'It was wonderful. What a helpful sermon the pastor preached. And to see all the Bibles!'

Courtney took a deep breath and pulled a Bible out of the purse that hung on a strap over her shoulder. 'Well, some people at church saw you staring at the Bibles. They thought maybe – well, that you didn't have a Bible in English, so they gave me this to give to you.' She pushed a new-looking Bible toward him.

Ivan's face burned with emotion. 'This is the richest gift anyone could give. But it is so much.'

Courtney looked puzzled. 'Ivan, I'm glad you like it, but it's only a Bible!'

Ivan stared at her in amazement. 'Only a Bible! What do you mean?'

Courtney looked embarrassed. 'I just mean – well – it's not – well, you don't have to act as if it's solid gold or something. Just take it!'

Ivan took the Bible in his hands. This Bible was his own. He felt as if God had secretly given him the one thing he wanted more than anything in the world. When he looked up at Courtney he was smiling with pleasure even though tears were caught in his lashes. 'Thank you, Courtney. You must thank your friends who gave this to me.'

Courtney stood up suddenly. 'Come on, Ivan,' she said, with the first smile she had ever given him. 'Let's walk outside.' Without looking back, she strode to the door.

'I have to tell Fedorchuk where I am,' Ivan protested. 'I'll only be a moment!' Ivan carefully tucked the Bible into the inside pocket of his jacket.

Outside, the September afternoon was hot and lazy. A mist hung over the trees in the distant hills. Golden leaves spun in the still air and floated to the earth.

'I want to tell you I'm sorry about something. I didn't believe that you could really be a Christian.' Courtney's voice was trembling. 'I thought that the Russian government would just send someone who would pretend to be a Christian. My Sunday school teacher said she doubted very much that the government would ever let a Christian come on an exchange program.'

'She is right. But Stephen Academy asked to have a believer in the group. That was one of the requirements.'

'I know. But I thought someone would be picked who would say he was a Christian when he really wasn't. But in church, when I saw you singing and listening to the sermon – and just now – about the Bible – well, I'm so sorry, Ivan.'

Ivan and Courtney were walking toward the chapel. The afternoon sunlight sifted through the branches of the trees around the chapel so that patches of light and dark mottled its white frame side. It was a beautiful sight. He felt a pang of regret as he realized he was disobeying the order to say nothing about Georgi.

Courtney listened quietly. Ivan wondered if she could understand why someone like Georgi would risk so much to stay in America. 'I don't even know why he is doing it,' Ivan finished. 'We had so little time to talk.'

Courtney was not surprised. 'If he had only a grandfather in Russia – and the grandfather wanted him to leave – well, of course, Georgi would try to stay. Everyone would want to live in America if they could.'

For a moment, both fell silent. Ivan considered telling Courtney that even if he didn't have Momma and Poppa and Katya at home, he would still want to go back to his own country. How could he explain his love of Russia, even though there were so many problems for believers in his country? He thought

longingly of the Moscow River winding through the city, the parks and statues he knew so well, Red Square and St. Basil's Cathedral – he decided to save all this for another conversation.

'I know where we can telephone!' Courtney's soft voice interrupted his thoughts. 'The library has a telephone on the librarian's desk. It's closed today, but one of the back windows has a loose lock. I know how to jiggle it so we can open a window. Come on!'

Slowly, so as not to arouse anyone's interest, they walked to the library and around the red brick building to the back. They came to a window that could be reached by standing on the low edge at its base. Courtney grabbed the bottom of the window on both sides and shook the window from side to side, watching the latch at the top. At just the right moment, when the latch flew open, she heaved the window up.

'If anybody sees us they'll wonder why anybody would be trying to get into the library,' she giggled. 'Usually we're trying to get out!'

They scrambled inside and Ivan closed the window carefully after them. The room was cool and dim after the bright sunlight. The smell of books and polished floors was pleasant, even though both children could hardly see in the shadowy room. Courtney walked swiftly to a desk at the other end of the room. Ivan followed, and they stopped beside a gleaming black telephone.

# An Urgent Telephone Call

Courtney ignored the telephone and pulled a directory off a shelf. 'The number for the FBI in New York should be in here.' Holding her thumb against the side of the fat directory, she spun through the pages until she came to the F's. Slowly, she scanned down the columns of numbers.

'You have a directory with every telephone?' Ivan marvelled. 'In Russia, people who have telephones do not have directories. They are available in the post office.'

'Here it is!' Courtney kept her finger on the number. 'I'll put the call through an operator so the operator can call back and let us know how much it costs. I do this a lot when I am calling home from a school phone and don't have my telephone card with me.'

Ivan didn't understand what she meant, but he kept silent. The important thing was to talk to the FBI for Georgi. Courtney spoke in a low voice to the operator. Ivan felt his stomach tense. Whether it was fear or excitement he didn't know. He tried to steady his voice in case the call did get through to the FBI. And in case someone was there on a Sunday.

Courtney suddenly thrust the telephone at Ivan. 'It's ringing!'

A calm male voice answered the phone. He sounded slightly surprised to receive a Sunday call.

Ivan's knees trembled. 'I am a Russian student studying in America,' he began.

'What is your name, please? We have been unable to contact you.'

Ivan shook his head quickly. 'Oh no! I am calling for a friend.'

'I see.' The voice was now cautious.

'My friend wants to stay in America but he needs some help. He doesn't know what to do.'

'Is your friend with you? Could I speak to your friend, please?'

'No! No – he is hiding. If you tell me what he should do, I will tell him.'

'He needs to come to our office in New York. Can he manage this?'

'Could someone come and get him? He has just arrived,' Ivan countered. 'I don't know if he could find his way to New York City.'

'That is not the best way. That might look as if he were taken against his will. Where is your friend? What is his name?'

Ivan hesitated. What if this man were not to be trusted?

'It is Georgi. Where in New York should he come?' Ivan reached for a pen that was on the desk. Courtney shoved a piece of paper toward him.

'Where are you calling from?' There was a slight note of insistence in the man's voice.

'Just tell me the address.' Ivan tried to keep the feeling of frustration out of his voice.

Two things happened at almost the same moment. The office door was flung open and Courtney pulled the phone smoothly away from Ivan and hung up.

'What is the meaning of this?' Comrade Fedorchuk's ordinarily white face had an angry flush of red on each cheek. Behind him, Mr. Bradley gazed at the children with an expression of concern on his face.

'I was showing Ivan how we make telephone calls in America.' Courtney noticed the open directory on the desk and flipped it shut. 'They don't have directories in Moscow, and Ivan was interested in how we telephone.' Courtney directed her answer to Mr. Bradley, avoiding Fedorchuk's blazing eyes.

'How did you get into the library, Courtney?' Mr. Bradley moved into the room and sat on the edge of the desk.

'I'm sorry, Mr. Bradley. I won't do it again – well, through the window. It's easy to free the lock. Lots of people do it, Mr. Bradley – when we don't get books back in time and the library is closed.'

Mr. Bradley walked over to the window and

examined the lock. 'This needs to be fixed,' he observed.

'This is outrageous!' Fedorchuk exploded at Ivan. 'You are a disgrace to Soviet youth! You behave like a common criminal, entering a locked building through a window, using school property –'

His speech was interrupted by the ringing of the telephone. The operator calling back! Ivan stared helplessly at Courtney. Courtney's eyes were upon Mr. Bradley who walked to the desk and picked up the receiver. After a few seconds he said, 'Thank you,' and quietly hung up the phone. Fedorchuk looked expectantly at Mr. Bradley who said nothing.

'Ivan will have to return to his room at once!' Fedorchuk pulled Ivan to the door. Mr. Bradley and Courtney followed, walking in silence behind them.

Back in his room, Ivan sat miserably on the edge of his bed. Fedorchuk paced back and forth on the small carpet by the door. Olga Drobovna turned the desk chair to face the bed and slumped slightly as she talked to Ivan, her posture revealing her fatigue.

'You must have been calling someone,' she insisted. 'It cannot be that you were merely learning to use an American telephone.'

'Courtney was showing me how to look up numbers in a directory and how to call an operator and how to dial. At home, I have never made a telephone call. My parents do not have a telephone in our Moscow flat.'

'But why? Why would you want to know how to telephone in America? Whom would you telephone?'

Ivan was praying as Olga Drobovna and Fedorchuk talked. 'Dear Lord, help me. Help me not to lie. Help me not to betray Georgi.'

'I know no one in America. Whom would I call?'

Fedorchuk stopped pacing and planted his feet apart on the rug. His eyes narrowed in threat. 'If you are playing some game with me – if you are lying, you will regret it for the rest of your life!'

A quiet peace came over Ivan. There was nothing Fedorchuk could ever do to him that the Lord didn't allow. It was the Lord who held his safety. Ivan relaxed.

'I promise you, comrades, I have not told you any lie. What I have told you is the truth. I know it was wrong to go into the library through the window, and I apologize sincerely.'

Olga Drobovna sighed and turned her head toward Fedorchuk. 'We have more important things to attend to, comrade, than Ivan Nazaroff and his little girlfriend.'

Ivan flushed but said nothing.

Fedorchuk glared at Ivan. 'You Christians are very crafty. Don't think I won't be watching you!'

I know you and Comrade Drobovna are watching one of us, Ivan thought.

'Don't think you are getting off without punishment!'

Comrade Drobovna stood up. Ivan felt a sting of pity for her. She looked very tired.

'We will talk with Mr. Bradley about this

situation,' she said, moving past Fedorchuk and opening the door. 'We will decide together with him what must be done about you and the American student. Tomorrow our classes begin. Try to stay out of trouble, Ivan. Any further trouble and it will be regrettable.'

Fedorchuk looked unhappy at the outcome of the conversation but he turned, after a final glare at Ivan, and followed Comrade Drobovna out. The door shut quietly behind them. Ivan jumped up from the bed and felt the door. It was not locked. Relieved, he sat down again on the bed. What a mess things were in! How could he help Georgi now?

# Shelter in the Storm

A soft knock on the door aroused Ivan. He had been praying on his bed and had dozed off. The room looked dim, as if it were evening. Guiltily, he sat up. The knock was repeated.

Stumbling to the door, he opened it awkwardly. Lida Ligachovna gave him a sweet smile. 'Olga Drobovna says that a group of us may walk to the village to buy ice cream. She and Fedorchuk are meeting with the school authorities about Georgi and what to do about his disappearance. Would you like to come? We can go if we promise to stay together and return immediately after we buy the ice cream. There is a little store open in the village today.'

I know the store, Ivan thought glumly.

'Well? Do you want to come?'

'What time is it?' Ivan squinted at his watch. 'Perhaps I have to stay in my room. I think I am in trouble.'

Lida shook her head. 'It's only four o'clock. The sun has gone in, that's all. And I asked if you might come, Ivan, and she said it was all right if we go right away. It looks as if it might rain later.'

Ivan pulled his jacket off the bed where he had thrown it and hurried with Lida to the small group waiting by the front door. In a minute, they were walking down the familiar road, excited not to be supervised.

Most of the talk all the way to the village revolved around Georgi. Several of the students thought he had run away to the city and would come back by evening.

'That will be the end of freedom for all of us,' Michael Semedi said glumly. As the oldest student, he was most concerned about his future and making a success of his time in America. He also kept to himself more than the others.

'I do not believe we will be punished for the actions of one extremely disloyal person. He is selfish! Only thinking of himself! That is not the Russian way. Did he ever stop to think of our group and how such stupidity might affect us all?' This was from Irina Kharchevna. Her usually soft voice rose in indignation. 'I have written to my parents about this. What he did will not be forgotten.'

Ivan felt cold. As he zipped up his jacket he felt his new Bible press against his chest. 'Perhaps he has reasons for what he has done,' Ivan suggested.

Josif Lamekin was striding quickly, his hands in his pockets. 'Whatever his reasons, he has not been logical. The effect of his actions will be serious.'

They were turning into the village. Ivan peered anxiously ahead to the entrance of the park. The day had grown so dark it was hard to see in the distance. 'It's going to rain,' Josif observed. 'A storm is coming!'

'Let's hurry and get our ice cream!' Lida urged.

The group began to half-run to the store. Ivan was relieved that their haste prevented anyone from glancing into the park as they passed. Ivan turned his head to look for Georgi, but all he glimpsed were bushes waving in the sudden wind. Thunder rumbled from far away.

'Was just about to close,' the shop-keeper remarked as the students burst into his store. He unlocked the cash register, then bent over the freezer where he scooped ice cream out of the bin. He showed no surprise at the appearance of the Russian students and solemnly handed an ice cream cone over the glass counter to each one.

'Storm's up,' he observed.

'Yes! We're going straight back to Stephen Academy. Do you think we'll make it before the storm?'

'Nope.' The shopkeeper relocked his cash register and hung the key on a little nail beside the counter. He followed the group out of the door just as a bolt of lightning crashed in the sky. From another place in the heavens, thunder growled. The wind had risen while they were in the store and whipped the girls' skirts about their legs.

The shopkeeper disappeared into a tiny car and drove around the corner, leaving the young people alone on the street. Lightning crashed again, brilliant in the almost darkened sky. Lida shuddered.

'We're going to get wet. Let's hurry!'

Vladimir Potopov was watching the gas station sign whipped about by the wind, crashing against its pole. 'This is a very bad storm. We should find shelter.'

'Where?' The questions was on everyone's lips. The street was deserted. Leaves fled wildly before the gusts of wind. Ivan felt panic about Georgi in the park. What if he ran out to find a safe doorway? Everyone would see him.

'Maybe the church is open!' Ivan shouted. 'Follow me!' He leaned into the wind, pushing against it as he struggled along the street. The students trailed behind, unsure of where he was leading them but willing to follow anyone with an idea. Just as the road turned, they came to the church. Leaves and papers swirled around the door.

'Is it open?' someone yelled over the thunder. In answer, Ivan yanked hard, pulling the door toward him with all his might. It opened so readily that he almost fell backwards. The rain was starting to fall in large drops as the students rushed into the silent building, slamming the door behind them with a mighty bang. For a moment they were breathless and laughing with the joy of a successful escape. Then they looked around, growing quiet in the soft light of small lamps along the side walls of the sanctuary that gave off a peaceful glow.

Sheets of rain beat against the windows. 'We're safe in here,' Luba Stepanova said in a hesitant voice.

'Yes,' Ivan smiled, thinking about the morning sermon.

Some of the students opened the hymn books and

Bibles in the pew racks. 'Look!' Josif exclaimed in astonishment. 'They use Bibles in here! I thought the Bible was no longer read in the modern world. It is very unscientific. It is full of mistakes.'

'How curious!' Lida picked up a Bible and sat down. 'Look at the first page!' she exclaimed. 'It starts out, 'In the beginning, God made the heavens and the earth.''

'See what I told you,' Josif answered, turning to the first page. 'Imagine such a thing! God made! And who is this God?'

Lida was busy reading. 'It doesn't say.'

Yuri Fedorov was sitting by himself in a pew at the front, ignoring the books. He snorted.

'But it does have the order of the natural world correct,' Lida said. 'It is just as the scientists say.'

Yuri pulled out a Bible. 'Let me see.' His voice was full of scorn. 'I would like to see how such a primitive book could contain correct science.'

Soon all the students were busy reading the first page of the Bible, exclaiming over the account of how the world was created. Ivan was watching his classmates with amazement. It was beyond his dreams. Here they were, thankful to be inside a church, each one bent over a Bible, earnestly discussing what they read.

Alexi finally turned to Ivan. 'How do you explain that, in the ancient times, before science was invented, someone could write down the correct order of creation? I think some modern person has gone over this page and corrected old mistakes.'

Ivan shook his head. 'The ancient documents have been preserved carefully down through the centuries. Not one word has been changed. Even our own Russian specialists know this is true. No believer would dare to change a word of the Bible.'

'Why not? We correct our old histories if they are wrong.' Yuri looked at his Bible with distaste.

'Because the Bible cannot be wrong,' Ivan began hesitantly. He knew the group would not like what he was going to say. 'The Bible was written by God Himself.'

At this the students laughed. Even Lida, who respected Ivan, laughed in spite of herself.

'Did God get a pen and write it in the clouds and then drop it on someone's head?'

Ivan selected his words prayerfully. 'God chose people to write the books of the Bible and He guided them and prevented them from writing anything wrong.'

Instead of laughing, there was an unexpected pause in the conversation. Then thunder broke almost overhead and a bright bolt of lightning sent a deafening crash into the room so that everyone

was shaken. New waves of rain swept across the windows. Silently, the group continued to read the Bibles. Ivan forced himself to sit still even though he was growing more and more agitated as he thought about Georgi in the stormy park.

Unheard in the storm that battered the small building, the inside door at the front of the church opened slowly and a shadowy figure moved as quietly as possible toward the students.

# The Accident

Ivan saw the figure first. He hesitated for a moment before rising slowly to his feet and making his way to the aisle at the end of the pew. With a tremendous sense of relief, Ivan recognized the pastor of the church.

The pastor was smiling broadly at the sight of the scattered group of young strangers intently reading Bibles.

'I hope it's all right.' As Ivan spoke, the group noticed the pastor. They dropped the Bibles hastily in the pew racks and stood uneasily where they were. 'We came in to get out of the storm.'

Suddenly the pastor recognized Ivan. 'Oh! You're the young Russian exchange student. Ivan, isn't it?'

'Yes. And these are some of the others in my group. We walked to the village for ice cream.'

The pastor moved to greet each student with a kindly handshake. 'Not the best weather for ice cream, is it? I'm very glad you took shelter in the church. It's an unusual storm for this time of the year, and it came up very fast.' As if to verify his words, a flash of brilliant lightning lit the windows at one side of the church. An almost deafening crash of lightning seemed to split the sky overhead. Ivan was gripped with worry about Georgi.

The pastor shook out a long yellow raincoat he was carrying. 'I wasn't sure all the windows of the church were shut after this morning's service. I came along to check. I was on my way to the education building when I heard your voices in the sanctuary.'

An idea struck Ivan. 'Please let me check the windows for you. I don't mind the storm.'

The pastor smiled reassuringly at the students and then turned his gaze back to Ivan. 'That's very kind of you. I'd like very much to spend a few minutes getting acquainted with your friends. And then perhaps I can drive you all back to Stephen Academy. It doesn't look as if this storm is going to let up soon.' The pastor held out his coat to Ivan. 'But you must take my raincoat.'

Ivan shrugged into the coat. As he hurried to the door of the sanctuary, the raincoat billowed behind him. He pushed the heavy door and almost fell into a wave of rain blown against the church by the high wind. Ivan turned and ran as hard as he could away from the church buildings and toward the park, blinded by the rain pelting onto his face and into his eyes.

As he reached the park he tried to shake the rain out of his eyes. For a moment he could see the bushes and trees swaying wildly in the storm. He shouted Georgi's name but his voice was drowned out by the beating of the rain and wind. Inside the park he stopped beside the bushes where he had left Georgi. Another flash of lightning made the small park as bright as day. Even before the crack of lightning,

Ivan could see the park was empty.

He ran back into the street and tried to see through the rain in all directions. The whole village seemed abandoned to the storm. Ivan turned back to the church, this time pushed along by the wind at his back. Gasping for breath, he gulped rain and air into his wet mouth as he ran to the low education building beside the church. Every window was shut tightly.

By the time Ivan fell back inside the church, he was soaked to the skin. The loose raincoat had done very little to keep him dry. Unbuttoning it with stiff fingers, he slipped it off and shook it slightly. Water poured from it onto the floor of the entrance way and dripped from Ivan's trousers. He pushed his soaking hair off his forehead, bundled the dripping coat under his arm and hurried into the church. He took two steps and lurched forward crazily as his feet slid out from under him. He crashed noisily to the floor.

'Ivan, are you all right?' The pastor hurried down the centre aisle of the church toward him.

'Oh yes!' Ivan blushed in embarrassment and lifted himself to his feet. A burning pain shot up his leg and Ivan fell back with a low moan.

The other students crowded around him. 'You have hurt yourself, Ivan. Stay still!' Lida Ligachovna was bending over him with concern. 'What hurts?'

The pastor untangled Ivan from the yellow raincoat and noticed that his face had whitened in pain. 'Well, I think I have just turned my ankle,' Ivan said tightly. 'I think it will be all right in few minutes.' Already he felt a burning throbbing in his foot.

The pastor helped Ivan up and seated him gingerly on a pew. 'While you were gone, Ivan, my wife called to tell me that the road is flooded a little way along toward Stephen Academy. I was just telling your friends that I'll drive them as far as I can in the church van. Where the road is flooded, they'll have to walk along the hill path by the roadside until they get to higher ground and road is passable. Mr. Bradley will be waiting in his van to pick them up. But you, young man, must see Doc Parker. You are in no condition to walk anywhere!'

Michael Semedi put Ivan's arm around his neck and pulled Ivan gently to his feet.

'Can you hop to the van, Ivan? If you can't we can easily carry you.' Ivan's wet trousers were sticking to his leg and he felt his swelling ankle pushing against his shoe.

'I can hop.' He tried to sound cheerful but his voice was strained and thin. The group moved slowly toward the back door of the church and out into the driving rain and wind. Pools of water flooded the parking lot. The students and the pastor ran for the van. Michael braced himself against the wind and walked steadily and slowly, supporting Ivan as he hopped and splashed through the puddles. Finally Ivan was settled in the front seat of the van next to the pastor.

The van edged into the dark street like a tall boat making its way through a storm at sea. Lida sat in the front next to the door, holding Ivan's injured foot in her lap. Ivan tried to see out of the front window of the van. The lights of the vehicle caught small flying branches in their arcs and lit up sudden curtains of rain.

Just beyond the bridge, the pastor eased the van over to the side of the road. 'Can you see that path that runs along the rise at the side of the road?' He addressed the question to Michael, as the oldest student in the group.

Michael pressed his face against the window of the van and peered into the storm. 'I think so,' he said hesitantly. Then with satisfaction he added, 'Yes, I do see it!'

'Good!' The pastor forced his door open and fought his way against the wind to the side of the van and slid the door open. 'You'll only need to walk a few minutes to get to higher ground at the top of a hill. This is the lowest place in the road. It always floods in a storm. Mr. Bradley will be waiting where the road is higher.'

'I'll explain that Ivan is at the doctor's,' Michael assured the pastor, 'and that you or Mr. Bradley will bring him to the academy as soon as you can.'

'Good!' The pastor smiled at the little group huddled together in the rain. 'Stay together and let Michael lead,' he called. 'You'll be back at Stephen Academy before you know it.'

# No Escape

A feeling of misery settled over Ivan as the van turned in the road and pulled away from the students climbing through the wind to the hillside path. Lida had waved bravely to Ivan and then was lost in a gust of rain. Ivan shivered and tried to hold his ankle as still as possible as they drove. Water had already risen to the hubcaps of the van as they crossed the bridge, heading back into town.

Somewhere out in the storm was Georgi. Now there was no way Ivan could even find him. He closed his eyes. 'God is our refuge and strength, a tested help in times of trouble. Let the oceans roar and foam; let the mountains tremble!' One of Poppa's favorite psalms came into his mind. Ivan felt too discouraged and in too much pain to pray. Instead he kept his mind on a few words from the psalm.

'We don't have far to go. Are you all right?' The pastor kept his eyes straight ahead on the road as he spoke to Ivan. 'I'm sorry I don't have a blanket in the van. I'm sure you're cold.'

'Thank you. I'm fine.'

The wind was dying down as the van pulled into a driveway by a white frame house. Lights in all the downstairs windows made golden blurs through the grey rain. Ivan and the pastor slipped and splashed up the veranda stairs. The pastor banged on the door with his free right hand in a fist. His left arm was supporting Ivan's weight.

The door opened quickly, and Ivan and the pastor were helped into the doctor's office in a small room off the front hall. The doctor was a young man with a slight build and calm hazel eyes. He smiled briefly at Ivan as he laid him on his leather couch and covered him with a warm brown blanket. The pastor introduced Ivan and explained how he hurt his ankle. The doctor probed the ankle gently. 'I'm pretty sure it's only a sprain, young man. We'll take an X-ray, just the same. Then I'll wrap it up for you and give you something for the pain.'

After the X-ray, the doctor's wife tapped on the door. She entered carrying a tray with mugs of steaming hot chocolate and a plate of oatmeal cookies. The doctor had given Ivan a pill to ease the pain of his ankle and had wrapped it snugly in an elastic bandage. An ice bag was held on the bandage by a small towel pinned at the top. Ivan was very surprised when the doctor bowed his head to thank God for the refreshments. The doctor's wife had brown braids pinned at the back of her neck, similar to the way Momma often wore her hair. Ivan felt a lump in his throat as he sipped the chocolate. The cookies were still warm from the oven, and Ivan ate three before he remembered his manners.

The doctor's wife laughed. 'My husband never eats fewer than six when cookies just come from the oven, Ivan. So you have three more to go!' As if to prove the truth of his wife's words, the doctor reached for another cookie and munched it happily.

'Ivan,' the doctor began, 'I'm sorry about your ankle and that we met in this way, but I have to tell you that it is very nice to meet a Christian from the Soviet Union. Doug here–' the doctor nodded toward the pastor, 'told me after church this morning about your being in the congregation. I didn't know we'd meet so soon, but I'm glad to know you.'

'Thank you.' Ivan noticed a worn Bible on the windowsill of the doctor's office. 'I didn't know I would meet other Christians in America. It is very strange for me to meet Christians so easily. Maybe I'm not explaining what I mean very well–'.

The pastor's wife poured Ivan another cup of hot chocolate. 'We understand, Ivan. We didn't expect to meet a Russian believer, either. But what a shame about your ankle on your first weekend in America!'

The rain was falling slowly now and the sky had lightened from dark to a silver grey. 'The storm's letting up,' the doctor said cheerfully. 'Perhaps the bridge will be passable in a while. I'm not sure, though, if you shouldn't think about staying put for the night. It's late already. Doug can call the school.'

For a few minutes, Ivan had forgotten about Georgi. A look of panic swept over his face. All three of the adults noticed it. 'Is it your ankle?' the doctor glance down at Ivan's foot.

'No!' Ivan answered quickly. He stopped,

confused, unsure of what to say. 'I mean, my ankle feels much better. Thank you.'

'But something is wrong.' The doctor's wife sat on the end of the leather couch. Ivan looked at her hopelessly.

'It's nothing that can be helped. I'm all right.' Ivan felt very tired. The warmth of the blanket and the hot chocolate, the rhythmic beating of the gentle rain and the easing of his pain worked together to overwhelm him with sleepiness.

He awoke to hear the pastor speaking quietly on the doctor's telephone. Without moving from the delicious warmth and comfort that encircled him, he listened sleepily to the pastor's voice. 'If he could stay the night, the doctor thinks the rest and staying off his feet would do him a lot of good. He's sleeping now. The doctor would like to keep an eye on his ankle. I could bring him well before class in the morning.'

The pastor pulled the blanket up around Ivan's chin before he walked softly out of the room and closed the door behind him. There were a few minutes of muffled conversation, and Ivan heard the front door close. The church van was started up and driven away. Ivan drifted back to sleep.

When he awoke again, the room was dark and the house silent. The doctor's wife had loaned him a warm sweater of her husband's, and Ivan sat up slowly on the couch, rolling the long sleeves of the sweater back over his wrists. Very gingerly he lowered his uninjured foot to the floor and then his sprained ankle. By taking the laces out of his shoe he managed to get his shoe on his injured foot.

'I've got to find Georgi.' There was a night-light on in the hallway. Ivan stood in the hall and heard voices speaking quietly upstairs. The hall clock said ten.

Ivan let himself out onto the porch. The night was mild, with a washed sky ablaze with stars that were reflected in the pools of water that stood on the lawn of the doctor's yard.

Hobbling painfully, Ivan worked his way to the road and turned toward the park. The night was peaceful after the fury of the storm. Water from the leaves of the trees dripped steadily into glistening puddles. Bushes still bent from the weight of the rain seemed to be drinking from the pools of water at their roots.

Too late Ivan heard the scrunching of car tires on the wet street. A police car slowed down beside him. A middle-aged officer poked his head out of the car. 'I don't believe I know you, young fellow.'

Ivan tried to fight down the unreasonable fear that choked him. 'I am just out for a walk.'

The officer glanced down at Ivan's bandaged ankle. 'Reckon a walk's not any too good for your foot there.' The police officer pulled back the emergency brake and got out of the car. 'What's your name, young man?'

'I am just out for a walk, doing nothing wrong.'

'You're one of those Russian students at Stephen Academy!' the officer declared.

Ivan nodded.

The officer opened the back door of the police car. 'Get in, please.'

Ivan stood on the side walk. 'But what have I done?'

The officer took Ivan's arm and helped him into the car.

'Just get in. I'm taking you to the station son. I have some questions to ask you.'

# Confession

The police captain was a small man who looked packed into his uniform. He walked with a stiff swagger as if he could not bend. Ivan watched him warily as he came out from behind a high desk and opened a gate to let Ivan and the officer pass into the police station. The police officer hovered near Ivan, ready to give him support if he stumbled with his sprained ankle. Ivan was surprised by the way the officers treated him. He had been in Soviet police stations and the KGB who investigated political or religious offences were never kind.

Ivan fought down a feeling of panic. It was unthinkable what Olga Drobovna and Yuri Fedorchuk would do when they found out he had been picked up by the American police! And now it seemed hopeless that he would find Georgi and be able to help him. Everything was wrong.

The officers stood aside at the door of a small room to let Ivan enter. As he limped toward a chair, a man standing by the window moved a little toward him. Ivan stared at him in astonishment: It was the same man who had been watching the Russian students at Saturday's football game! Ivan couldn't hide the surprise that registered on his face.

The man sat down beside a table in the room.

He smiled reassuringly at Ivan. 'Please don't be concerned. You have done nothing wrong. We just want to ask you some questions. I believe you noticed me at the football game, if you remember?'

Ivan nodded grimly. Police always began by saying they were just asking some questions. The KGB in Moscow, when trying to trap someone, would begin in such a way. Silently Ivan prayed for God's help. He eased himself onto a chair, his eyes never leaving the face of the man in the grey suit.

'I am from the FBI,' he began. 'The Federal Bureau of Investigation. Do you know about the FBI?'

Ivan's mind flashed to Georgi's desperate face in the park – 'I tried to call the FBI in New York...' – and to his own call later. 'I have heard of it,' Ivan answered slowly.

'Last Friday night the FBI received a recorded telephone message. It was from a Russian student who said he wished to defect. Then early this afternoon, a second call received, but it was cut off.'

'I have no wish to defect!' Ivan exclaimed. 'I came to the village with my comrades when the storm began. I sprained my ankle and was taken to the doctor. There I must spend the night. I am going back to Stephen Academy in the morning, as soon as the roads are safe. I – was out walking, that was all.'

The FBI agent looked thoughtful. 'You sprained your ankle. And then you went out for a walk?'

Ivan flushed and was silent.

The agent folded his arms and leaned back in his chair. 'The FBI does not handle defections to the West unless the persons wishing to stay have significant scientific or military information that would be useful. The FBI is not the agency concerned. It is usually a matter for the immigration service. We are, however, willing to help.'

'But I do not wish to stay in the West!' Ivan thought of Momma and Poppa and Katya. 'I want to go home after the weeks of my study are over! My parents and little sister are in Moscow.'

The FBI agent nodded understandingly and sighed. 'Please try not to be afraid. I want to help. But I have a little problem here. We get a call from a Russian student. It is not difficult to check out who has recently arrived from the Soviet Union. Your group is the only one anywhere close to New York. I am assigned to keep an eye on this group to see if anyone appears to be trying to make contact. Everything seems quite normal, but our office gets another call today. And now the officer comes across a Russian student, alone, with a sprained ankle, out for a walk at ten o'clock at night, miles from Stephen Academy. Perhaps you can see my problem.'

'You could really help such a student who wanted to stay in America?'

The FBI agent gazed at Ivan. 'Such a student should be advised that it is a very serious step. That if such a student formally requested to remain in the United States, he might never be able to return to his own country.'

'But you could help him? You could prevent Soviet officials from forcing him to return home?'

'Yes. We could do that. If such a person had very carefully considered that he might never again see his mother or father or – sister.'

Ivan looked out of the small window in the room. An iron grating covered the glass. All that could be seen at the window was the deep black of the night. Ivan could pretend to know nothing. That way he would be safe from the certain punishment he would receive if Comrades Drobovna and Fedorchuk found out that he had tried to help Georgi. After all, it was nothing to him. Georgi wasn't a believer. Ivan thought about Poppa and what he would do. He often reminded the children that the Bible teaches believers to do good to all people – that by showing God's love to unbelievers, many come to know the love of God..

But was it right that Georgi was trying to defect? Perhaps he would be helping Georgi do something that was wrong! Perhaps helping him was wrong!

The FBI agent stood up slowly. 'Maybe you would like to go back to the academy now. The police will take you, and nothing will be said about our conversation.'

Georgi's words flashed into Ivan's memory. 'You Christians – you're supposed to help everybody, aren't you? Doesn't your religion say that you have to help people?'

'It is not I who wishes to leave Russia,' Ivan's voice was low and uncertain. 'It is not I, but I know who it was who telephoned and left the message. I have told him I would try to help him.'

The agent sat down again. He shook his head. 'How did you manage to get away from the group then? I know you must all stay together.'

The story was told in a few minutes. The FBI agent was concerned to learn that Comrades Drobovna and Fedorchuk knew Georgi was missing. 'If they find him before I do,' the agent remarked, 'It will be all over for him. There is nothing I can do at that point. Your friend will be on a plane back to Moscow before you can blink an eye.'

'I was supposed to meet him at the chapel after ten o'clock. Maybe he made it back to Stephen Academy before the storm.' Ivan looked hopefully at the agent.

'And you are supposed to be spending the night at Dr. Parker's?'

Ivan nodded.

'First we'd better call him and let him know where you are. It won't do to have him worrying about you if he notices you're missing.'

An officer slipped out of the room to make the call.

'It wouldn't be good for me to drive around the village with you in the car, Ivan. If Georgi sees a car, he's sure to hide. And you're in no condition to roam around yourself.' The agent puckered his lips in thought.

'Could we go back to the academy and look for Georgi at the chapel?'

'It's almost impossible that he could have made it back in the storm.'

'But he had to get there. That was the only plan we had!' Ivan's ankle was beginning to throb painfully. He guessed that the pain pill was wearing off.

'We'd have to park on the main road away from the school so we wouldn't attract attention. Your Russian teachers mustn't catch sight of you in a police car. Do you think you could walk down the long road to the academy on that foot?'

Ivan smiled gamely. 'I'll make it. I have to – it is the only plan we had!'

# Caught at the Chapel

Although the police officer looked squashed behind the wheel of the squad car, he drove with surprising ease, turning the wheel with one beefy hand while his other arm rested along the back of the passenger front seat. The FBI agent, looking like a businessman in his three-piece suit, peered into the darkness as they drove.

Ivan sat in the back seat praying silently. His ankle hurt. He was cold. As much as he tried, he couldn't shake off an unreasoning fear of the police that had been born thousands of miles away in his beloved Moscow. There, authorities could never be trusted. They represented the force of a state that was determined to get rid of any religious faith. Here it is different, Ivan kept telling himself. But it was dark in the back of the car, and he felt alone and lonely.

For some reason, an ancient orthodox prayer came into his mind. A grandmotherly cleaning lady at school muttered the prayer constantly as she swept the long street around the school property. She would repeat the prayer reverently aloud if anyone asked her, and Ivan had seen children at school mocking her prayer. Ivan liked it. Now it circled around in his mind and heart. 'Lord Jesus Christ, Son of God, have mercy on me a sinner. Lord Jesus Christ, Son of God, have mercy on me a sinner.' Ivan felt he was praying for Georgi, for Olga Drobovna, for Yuri Fedorchuk, for himself. All sinners in the world were included in his prayer.

The police officer had turned off the headlights of the squad car. Skillfully, he slowed down and brought the car to a silent halt on the side of the road. 'This is as far as we go. Let's get out and close the doors as quietly as we can.'

Ivan and the FBI agent obeyed wordlessly. The FBI agent leaned against the front fender. 'If Georgi sees a police officer or me, he won't come out of wherever he might be hiding – assuming, which I do not, that he is on the grounds.'

'He has to be!' Ivan said again.

The agent shrugged and went on. 'I'll stay by the car. I think it would be best, officer, if we both stayed close to the car, so that if Ivan does find him and brings him here, we can leave immediately. We may need to hurry.'

The officer nodded.

'Can you make it down the road and up the hill to the chapel?'

'I have to!' Even though he whispered the men heard the fierce determination in his voice.

'Is Georgi a special friend of yours, son?' the officer asked suddenly.

'No, I just met him on this trip.'

'Then why are going through so much to help him?' The officer took off his hat and scratched his head. 'Seems to me you could get yourself in a lot of trouble!'

'Yes.' Ivan didn't want to talk. He wanted to get away from the police car and get to the chapel. Yet both men were waiting for him to answer. 'I am helping him because he asked me. It is the law of Jesus Christ that we Christians help others who ask. And I know also what it is to fear. Georgi is very afraid.' Ivan paused for a moment. Neither man spoke. 'I will come back as soon as I can – with or without Georgi.'

It was easier and quieter to walk on the grass along the side of the road. The grass was slippery, and Ivan stumbled and limped along as quickly as he could. His injured leg became heavier and heavier as he moved so that by the time he came in sight of Stephen Academy, he was dragging his leg behind him. He was panting from pain and effort and he tried to smother his gasps in the upturned collar of his coat. Going up the hill toward the chapel, the sound of his heavy breathing and uneven staggering seemed loud enough to be heard easily from the school. His heart was pounding in fear. 'Lord, let Georgi be here. Let him see me and come out. Lord -!'

Ivan leaned against the side of the chapel and tried to quiet his breathing and his heart. The sound of water dripping from the many trees seemed to make a din in his ears. The strangeness of America almost overwhelmed him. 'Lord!' he pleaded again. A night breeze cooled his face and the heightened splashing of the water returned to normal. Ivan took a slow deep breath and felt a lightness within him. He felt hopeful.

'Georgi!' he whispered cautiously. 'Georgi! It's Ivan. Georgi, I'm here – it's Ivan.'

There was a sudden rustle of a bush, and a dark figure darted toward Ivan. 'I knew you'd come!'

Ivan strained to see Georgi's face in the faint starlight. He was grinning in relief although he looked haggard. 'Did you bring anything to eat?'

'Sorry. I'm so glad you're here!'

'What took you so long? Did you reach the FBI? Wasn't the storm terrible?'

'How did you get here?' Ivan was looking around carefully. The lights in many of the windows of the main building warned that people were still up and looking for Georgi.

'The bridge was flooded – I had to swim. The water was over my head, but I made it. I had to get here!'

Ivan smiled. 'I knew you would. Now all we have to do is make it back to the road. The FBI man is waiting for you!'

Georgi clutched Ivan in joy. 'Truly?'

'Yes! Only I have to go with you back to the village. I'm supposed to be staying there at the doctor's house because I hurt my ankle.'

Georgi looked admiringly at Ivan. 'You'd make a good KGB agent, comrade. What a fine story!'

'No!' Ivan protested more loudly than he intended. 'I really did sprain my ankle, and I would never be a KGB agent!'

Georgi laughed. Ivan could see he was becoming almost giddy with happiness. 'Of course not! But come on! You can lean on me.'

Ivan had just slung his arm over Georgi's shoulder when he froze in fear. Coming from the other side of the chapel, around to the back of the building were unmistakable footsteps moving swiftly across the grass.

Georgi had heard it too and froze. 'Can you run?' he whispered to Ivan.

Ivan shook his head. 'You run. I'll stay here!'

Georgi was silent then pulled Ivan back into the shadows. 'No. If you are found here, and I escape, you will be in great trouble.'

The footsteps slowed down and seemed to proceed with caution. Georgi pulled Ivan's arm back around his shoulder and grasped his hand hard.

'We've got to run!' As Georgi moved away from the side of the chapel, making for the cover of the trees that lined the road below, he slipped on the wet grass. Ivan pitched forward and fell with a cry of pain. Georgi bent over him to pull him to his feet and slipped again, falling almost on top of Ivan.

As both boys struggled to get up, a voice cut into the night. 'Ivan! And Georgi – just the person I was looking for!' It was Olga Drobovna.

# Five Minutes
# to Freedom

'Go!' Ivan muttered desperately. 'Run!'

'No! Not without you! They'll never believe you weren't in this with me. Come on, Ivan! You can make it!'

Olga Drobovna appeared beside them seemingly from out of nowhere. In a flash she grasped Georgi firmly by the wrist. 'I wouldn't advise you to run, young man. Comrade Fedorchuk is also looking for you. One call and he would be here in a moment.'

The teacher noticed Ivan trying to steady himself on his good foot. She peered at his injured ankle without letting go of Georgi. 'So the story about your sprained ankle was true.'

'Of course! The pastor called you, didn't he?'

'He told me you had sprained your ankle. Whether or not it was a lie, I could not know until I saw you. Now we will go inside and see what is to be done with you both.'

'Please let Georgi go, Olga Drobovna.' Ivan had hobbled over to a nearby tree. He leaned against the trunk wearily.

Olga Drobovna laughed. 'Go where? There is no place around here for him to go! And I suppose you don't wish to go with him, Ivan?'

'No! I want to go home to Moscow. To my family.

But Georgi has no family except his old grandfather. And there is a way for him to escape! There is an FBI agent waiting for him – somewhere...' Ivan's voice trailed off. Perhaps he shouldn't have told her so much.

'All the agents in the world cannot help him here. Not so far away from a city. Not on a Sunday night. It is quite hopeless. Come on!' She continued to hold Georgi's wrist.

'Come with me, Ivan!' As Georgi called out the words, he gave a desperate pull away from Olga Drobovna. In a powerful movement too quick to see, she pulled Georgi's arm behind his back in a crippling hold. Georgi cried out in pain.

'Comrade Drobovna,' Ivan began again, 'at the end of the road, just on the side of the highway, the FBI man and a police officer are waiting for Georgi. You could let him go. It might be a black mark for you when we get home, but it is his whole life.'

Olga Drobovna forced Georgi to kneel on the grass. She bent beside him. Her voice was very low. 'This is a trick. You are trying to trap me. This whole thing has been a KGB trick to test me.'

'I don't know what you are talking about! Let go of my arm!' Georgi's voice was thin with pain.

Comrade Drobovna trembled with anger. 'There is no FBI man! There is no police officer! You are wearing a microphone to trick me into saying I will let you go.'

'No, Comrade Drobovna! No! Georgi really does want to defect. He has no microphone!'

'And how clever you have been, little Christian. Going to church this morning and pretending to listen so intently. You are like all the Christians. You have learned to be secretive.'

Ivan felt uneasy. Something odd was happening that he didn't understand. Why hadn't Olga Drobovna called Fedorchuk as soon as she caught Georgi? She would only have needed to shout. Her voice would have easily carried through the quiet night. Why did she fear a trick? Why was she talking with them beside the chapel instead of immediately forcing them down the hill and into the bright lights of Stephen's?

'Comrade Drobovna, you know that Christians do not lie,' Ivan began. 'I promise you that the FBI man and a police officer are just down the road. I told them I would bring Georgi to the car if I found him. You can go down and look for yourself. They will not leave without me. They will take me back to Dr. Parker's house for the night.'

'So you have everything arranged, do you, Ivan?'

'No, comrade. But I noticed that you did not call Comrade Fedorchuk when you found us. I think you might have another reason for asking about the FBI man.'

'What is that?' She spoke so sharply that Ivan looked over his shoulder to see if Fedorchuk had heard and might be coming to find her.

'Comrade Drobovna, we have no microphones or instructions to get you into trouble. It is only a

125

five-minute walk to the police car. Five minutes to freedom.'

Comrade Drobovna let go of Georgi's arm and stood up, helping him to his feet. Georgi stood uncertainly, looking at Ivan. The teacher was staring intently at Ivan. Ivan wished the dark did not obscure her eyes. He could not tell what she was thinking.

'He is waiting for Georgi.' Ivan took a deep breath. 'Or anybody.'

Olga Drobovna pushed Georgi in front of her. 'Go!' she commanded in a low urgent voice. 'I will say you got away from me if you are lying and there is no car.'

Georgi stumbled forward and turned to Ivan in amazement. 'What will you do? Are you coming?'

Ivan smiled widely. Even in the dark, Georgi could hear the happiness in his voice. 'You go ahead, Georgi. I will come in a moment with Comrade Drobovna. Be careful you don't run into Fedorchuk!'

Still uncertain for an instant, Georgi turned and ran down the hill, keeping to the cover of the trees.

Olga Drobovna offered her arm to Ivan. Gratefully he hung on and the two of them made their way more slowly behind Georgi.

After a moment, she said, 'Why do you think I would go with Georgi?'

With every hop of his good leg, a shock of pain thudded in his ankle. Ivan longed to let go of Olga Drobovna's arm and sink to the grass. Yet he knew he had to get back to the car and return to the doctor's home to keep himself out of suspicion. 'You didn't call Fedorchuk – I saw you wanted to know Georgi's plan before we went inside the school.'

Olga Drobovna kept turning her head quickly from side to side, twisting around to look behind them as she hurried Ivan down the hill. 'There have been increasingly frequent questions about my loyalty – I have not been sufficiently political. This is my last trip. After this I will never get out again. I have seen that America is free – in a way we can't even dream about in Russia. I can't live anymore without this freedom – I had planned to defect on this trip – I didn't know the opportunity would come so quickly.'

As they approached the car, Georgi moved nervously toward the FBI agent when he saw Olga Drobovna approaching with Ivan. Ivan saw the questioning look on the faces of the two men. 'It's all right,' he gasped. 'Comrade Drobovna also wants your protection.'

The FBI agent moved toward her and held out his hand. Olga Drobovna shook it. 'You have thought carefully about this move, madam? Once you get in this car, there is no turning back without serious consequences to you.'

Olga Drobovna was smiling in a way Ivan had not seen before. 'Thank you! Oh, thank you! I have thought about this for a very long time.'

The police officer squeezed himself behind the wheel without a word. Olga Drobovna and Georgi got in the back seat and made room for Ivan. Painfully he eased himself in. As soon as the back seat door was shut, the police car eased onto the highway and sped toward town.

The clock on the church's steeple was chiming the hour of midnight when Ivan was helped out of the police car by Dr. Parker. He glanced at the other two passengers with curiosity. 'The teacher, too!' he said in surprise.

The officer shrugged and shook his head. Nothing like this had ever happened before. His expression seemed to say, I'm only driving the car.

Ivan's good-byes were filled with pain and uncertainty. It was hard to believe what was happening.

'I will miss our mother Russia!' Olga Drobovna said as she shook Ivan's hand.

Ivan suddenly remembered the engraved spoon Katya had given him before he left. Quickly he pulled it out of his pocket. 'Here is a remembrance from home,' he said as he thrust it into her hands.

Tears filled Olga Drobovna's eyes. 'But I can give you nothing.'

'Nor I!' declared Georgi. 'And you have been more than a friend to me.'

'One thing you can do.' The pain seemed to lift for a moment. 'Please – I don't know how to say it – but please, you will be free to look for God – find other Christians, and they will help you to know Jesus!' Both Olga Drobovna and Georgi looked bewildered and embarrassed. With a wave to Dr. Parker, the officer turned the key in the ignition and the noise of the car starting up broke the awkward moment.

Olga Drobovna looked down at Katya's spoon twinkling in her hand. 'I will remember,' she said softly. 'I also remember what the pastor said this morning: 'Jesus stills the storms of life.''

Georgi waved to Ivan as the car pulled away. He rolled down the window. 'Thank you, Ivan! I will remember what you said! I will!' The car turned out of the drive and was gone.

Dr. Parker helped Ivan into the house. As Ivan's head sank into a pillow, he smiled contentedly. For all of them, however different the ways, the American journey was about to begin!

Find out how it all began with Ivan's first adventure: Ivan and the Moscow Circus. Here is sneak preview of the first chapter of that book.

# A Chance Meeting

There was a pleasant slamming of compartment doors all up and down the train. The shrill whistle of the platform man signalled the 'all clear' for the train to resume its slow journey toward Moscow.

Ivan leaned back against his seat with a slight smile and closed his eyes. He was pretending to be a seasoned traveller, weary with the routine of the journey, a trifle bored with the delay of the train as it stopped at small villages to pick up a chance passenger or two.

Actually he was loving every minute of the journey and was glad there was still a long way before pulling into Yaroslavsky Station in Moscow where Momma and Poppa and Katya would be waiting to greet him.

It wasn't a journey he had wanted to make. A courtesy visit to distant relatives hadn't seemed like much fun when Momma and Poppa suggested it, but it had been a long time since Poppa's family in Vologda had been visited. A new baby had been born to a cousin Ivan didn't even remember, and Momma wanted to send along a special gift for the baby's first birthday.

At first the whole family had planned the journey together, but in the end it was decided that Ivan would go alone. Poppa did not receive permission from his supervisor at the factory to have time away from his job, and Momma's factory's quota was increased so that there was extra production and longer hours to work in order to reach the goal. Katya begged to be allowed to go with Ivan but Momma was firm.

'You would be too restless on the long journey, Katya. And it is too much responsibility for Ivan to keep you out of trouble.'

Katya folded her arms indignantly and looked so innocently outraged that everyone laughed. Finally, even Katya smiled and plopped into a chair, playfully pouting at having been made to change her mood.

'I do not get into trouble!' she declared from the depths of the chair. 'It's possible that things happen to me from time to time, but that is the result of a lively and inquisitive nature.'

'Oh, indeed?' Momma tilted her chin at Katya thoughtfully.

'Yes!' came the muffled insistence. 'My teacher Valentina Semionovna says it is a fine thing to have a lively and inquisitive nature.'

'She didn't think it so fine when you got lost at

the Science Exhibit,' Ivan declared, giving one of Katya's fat braids a pull. 'I didn't hear her praising you then!'

A pillow came flying from the chair, barely missing Momma's prized samovar on a table by the couch. Momma caught the pillow with a shake of her head. It was best for Ivan to make the journey alone.

Ivan felt the train lurch to a start. At the same moment, the compartment door opened and a battered suitcase was pushed through the door, followed by a boy Ivan's age. Ivan sat up straight with a smile.

'Hello!'

The strange boy hoisted his suitcase to the overhead rack, sat down on the bench opposite Ivan, and arranged his plastic bag of food on the side of the seat away from Ivan before answering.

'Hello.' He immediately stared out of the window.

Ivan continued to look at him for a moment. The boy was nicely dressed and had slightly long hair. He had a smooth complexion and lustrous dark eyes. Perhaps he is from Georgia, Ivan guessed.

The boy looked sad or sullen. Ivan couldn't decide which, but he began to feel uncomfortable at the boy's silence.

'Going to Moscow?' Ivan asked.

The boy turned his head to Ivan. 'Of course.'

Ivan shrugged. 'Me too.'

The boy was looking out of the window again.

'My name's Ivan. Ivan Sergeivich Nazaroff.'

The boy continued to gaze out of the window for so long Ivan was afraid he wasn't going to speak again at all. Finally with a sigh, he turned his head again. 'I am Volodia Petrovich Dyomin.'

Ivan smiled encouragingly, but Volodia turned again to the window. Ivan shifted in his seat uneasily. His companion clearly did not wish to talk. It was obvious he wanted to keep to himself. Such unfriendly behavior in a Soviet train was so unusual Ivan began to regret that the boy had come to his compartment. People always passed the time on trains talking, laughing, eating together. Another person in your compartment meant a new acquaintance, the exchange of stories, the sharing of meals, someone with whom to enjoy the passing view.

It's a good thing Katya isn't here, Ivan thought, wishing suddenly she were. She would have filled up the silence with many questions. Katya would have paid no attention to Volodia's unsociability. Of course if Momma were here, she would have restrained Katya, whispering to leave the boy alone. Then, Ivan knew, Momma would have silently prayed.

Ivan looked more closely at Volodia. Although

his body was tense, Ivan could see he was athletic and sat with an uneasy grace. A slight frown was creasing his forehead and from his profile, his sad expression seemed anxious, as if he were thinking very hard about a difficult situation.

Ivan leaned back again against his seat and closed his eyes. 'You can always pray, son.' How many, many times had he heard Poppa say those words? From as early as he could remember, in times of disappointment or frustration or worry, when it was true that nothing at all could be done about some problem in the church, some sorrow at school, some injustice, Poppa's advice was the same. As Ivan prayed, he could sense Volodia relaxing. He shifted and sighed and Ivan could hear him changing his position. When Ivan opened his eyes again, the boy was looking at him.

Ivan smiled.

Volodia nodded.

Ivan took a deep breath and sat up. 'I think it must be time to eat!'

'Of course,' Volodia agreed politely. 'I ate just before coming to the train. But you have been travelling a long time?'

'Four or five hours. From Volgda.'

Ivan opened the large bundle of food his Aunt Sophia had carefully wrapped in newspaper for him.

There was a large chunk of black bread and some cheese, hard-boiled eggs, sausages, and a tightly capped bottle of mineral water. Ivan offered the bundle to Volodia. Volodia shook his head quickly. 'Truly, I ate just a little while ago.'

Ivan paused to thank the Lord for the food and for the new friendliness of Volodia. 'Let me help him, Lord, if I can,' he prayed.

'Well, go on! Don't hesitate on my account. Really, I have just eaten,' Volodia encouraged.

Ivan took a bite of bread and chewed it thoughtfully. 'Are you going to Moscow to take part in some sports event?'

The boy laughed, his face lighting. 'No. Why do you ask that?'

'I thought you looked athletic. I play soccer and hockey for my school.'

Volodia nodded his respect. 'So you are how old?'

'Almost thirteen.'

'Ah. A loyal Young Pioneer, of course?'

Ivan suppressed surprise at the question, although he was suddenly on guard. Why would Volodia ask if he were a member of the Communist Young Pioneers? Almost every student in Russia, except those disqualified because of misbehavior or children with religious beliefs, belonged to the organization.

As a Christian, Ivan had never belonged, in spite of the pressure of his teachers. But it was most unusual for a passing acquaintance to mention such a thing.

Ivan shrugged casually. 'Well, that's a good question.' It was an evasive answer showing he didn't want to discuss it.

'No?' Volodia looked suddenly interested. 'You are not a Young Pioneer, I think, yet you are in sports? Something wrong?'

Ivan smiled. 'Nothing is wrong. At least, not with me. But you are right. I am not a Young Pioneer.'

Volodia shot out the next question. 'Why not?'

Poppa and Momma had taught Ivan that the Bible instructs Christians to be ready to give an answer to anyone about their faith. A direct question requires a direct witness. 'Although it is against the law to try to persuade people to be Christians, it is always permitted to answer questions,' Poppa would say.

Ivan paused a moment to choose his words carefully. 'Well, you know how it is. I am a believer.'

Volodia's dark eyes were alive with curiosity. 'A believer?'

'In God. In Jesus Christ. A Christian.'

There was silence in the compartment as Volodia thought about what Ivan had said. His response came slowly. 'I thought only old women...' His voice trailed off. Volodia frowned, bit his lip and started again. 'I've heard about religious believers.' He dropped his voice. 'I've heard such people still exist in our Soviet society, although they are mostly old women. But sometimes they are not.'

Ivan grinned. 'As you see,' he said.

Volodia did not return Ivan's smile. 'Is it true that sometimes religious believers are sent to prison camps or to hospitals for the insane?'

Ivan began to feel frightened. How could an ordinary boy like Volodia know such things unless he had some contact with the Secret Police?

Volodia suddenly stood up and pulled his suitcase down from the overhead rack. 'See this?' he asked brightly, pointing to an emblem sticker on his suitcase. It looked familiar and Ivan bent forward to read it.

'I am a member of the circus,' Volodia declared proudly.

Ivan was amazed.

'Have you never gone to the circus?' Both boys were staring at each other in mutual surprise.

'No.' Ivan tried to be tactful. 'It is not the custom for believers to go to the circus. But I have sometimes wished to go.'

Volodia heaved his suitcase back on the shelf and sat down.

Ivan offered him some cheese and this time Volodia accepted. Ivan cut off a chunk with his pocket knife and handed it to Volodia with a question. 'What do you do in the circus?'

'I am an acrobat. And I sometimes help in the clown acts.' Volodia wiped his mouth with the back of his sleeve. A look of sadness passed over his face. He looked as if he wanted to say something. Ivan waited. 'I didn't mean anything by the question about your not being a Young Pioneer,' he said finally. 'I'm not crazy about the organization myself. In fact, even though I am fifteen, I'm not a member of the Komsomol.'

'Why not?' It was Ivan's turn to risk a question.

Volodia gave Ivan a steady look. 'Should I tell you everything about myself?'

'I told you I am a believer.'

Volodia raised a quizzical eyebrow in agreement. 'Let us say perhaps there are those in my family who have some differences with the politics of our government.'

Ivan glance out of the window. A surge of appreciation for the openness of his new friend warmed him. Outside, the pale spring green of the central Russian plains slipped effortlessly by. A turn of the head to the compartment door showed it was tightly closed.

When Ivan made no answer, Volodia continued. 'Especially an uncle of mine. An uncle I love very much.'

Ivan reached out to touch Volodia's arm. 'I am sorry.'

Tears glistened in Volodia's eyes. His voice was so low Ivan had to lean forward in his seat to catch what Volodia was saying.

'Is it true what I have heard about some religious people? Sometimes they are sent away...'

Ivan interrupted quickly. 'Yes. Sometimes...'

'In camps?'

Ivan nodded. 'Only certain very active leaders. Or believers who are outspoken. Or sometimes it is just a matter of an official who wishes to pass his time making trouble for some believer.'

Volodia stared hard at Ivan. 'And in hospitals? Are Christians ever sent to psychiatric hospitals...' His voice was a whisper. '...for the insane? When they are not – insane in the least?'

Tears now flooded Volodia's eyes. Embarrassed, he looked out of the window as he regained composure.

Ivan leaned over in his seat and grasped Volodia's shoulder. 'I understand, my friend. It is your uncle who has been put in such a place. But why?'

'He has criticized the government. He has had

## CHRISTIAN FOCUS PUBLICATIONS

**Christian Focus** **Christian Heritage** **CF4K** **Mentor**

Christian Focus Publications publishes books for adults and children under its three main imprints: Christian Focus, Mentor and Christian Heritage.

Our books reflect that God's word is reliable and Jesus is the way to know him, and live for ever with him. Our children's publication list includes a Sunday school curriculum that covers pre-school to early teens; puzzle and activity books.

We also publish personal and family devotional titles, biographies and inspirational stories that children will love. If you are looking for quality Bible teaching for children then we have an excellent range of Bible story and age specific theological books.

From preschool to teenage fiction, we have it covered!

**Find us at our webpage:**
**www.christianfocus.com**

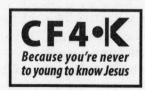

# THE IVAN SERIES

These books will have you on the edge of your seat as you enter a different world of just 30 years ago… but a world that isn't that different.

### *Ivan and the Moscow Circus*
Read how a key, a car, a foreign journalist and a clown suit help Ivan in one of his greatest adventures.

### *Ivan and the Daring Escape*
Ivan is trying to outwit the Secret Police, his skill at football helps him and his friends to get the better of them.

### *Ivan and the Informer*
Ivan refuses to join the Communist Youth organizations. He is taken for questioning and knows there is an informer somewhere – how can he clear his name?

### *Ivan and the Hidden Bible*
Ivan's not the most popular boy in school but he's the best footballer! Will he and Katya find the Bible that once belonged to their Grandfather?

### *Ivan and the Secret in the Suitcase*
Here are Ivan and Katya in another adventure – Smuggling! Can they outwit the secret police?

### *Ivan and the American Journey*
Ivan has won a prize in history and travels to the USA. It is a journey full of adventure and intrigue.

# IVAN SERIES

Before these books were written Russia was a communist country, which meant that belief in God and meeting together to worship him were strictly forbidden. Because of this, Russian Christians had to meet in secret. They had to be very careful of what they said and whom they trusted. Otherwise they could face arrest, interrogation, imprisonment, torture and sometimes even death.

As you read these books you will learn the meaning of some Russian words such as:

| | |
|---|---|
| **Babushka** | Grandmother |
| **Tovarisch** | Comrade or friend |
| **Kopeks/rubles** | Russian money |
| **Pravda** | Russian Newspaper |
| **Piroshki** | Small, meat-filled rolls |
| **Lobio** | Spicy red beans |
| **Borscht** | Soup |

**The Young Pioneers** were the Communist Party organization which provided all camping, athletic, musical and cultural activities for Soviet children aged 9-14.

The initials **KGB** were the initials of Russian Secret Police.

terrible trouble. Interrogations. Lost his job. And now…they have taken him to a special hospital where he is without rights. Possibly they are giving him treatments.'

Volodia stood up again and paced briefly in the swaying compartment. When he sat down his face was hard. 'But you could not understand what it is like to have someone you love in such a place.'

Memories flooded Ivan's mind. Volodia stared at Ivan's face.

'You do know,' he said softly.

Ivan smiled faintly in resignation. 'I do know. Once a pastor I loved was taken away to such a place.'

'Yet you smile.'

Ivan answered slowly. 'For believers, too, it is very hard. But for us, it is also an honour. Only the best of us suffer in these ways for Jesus Christ.'

A playful grin flitted over Volodia's face.

'Jesus Christ? But really, Ivan, isn't he a mythological character?'

Underneath the train, sparks flew as steel streaked across steel. In the compartment above, Ivan began to talk.